POETRY OF MID-CENTURY

1940–1960

POETRY OF MID-CENTURY 1940-1960

❖

EDITED AND WITH AN INTRODUCTION BY

MILTON WILSON

❖

GENERAL EDITOR : MALCOLM ROSS

A NEW CANADIAN LIBRARY ORIGINAL NO. 04

McClelland and Stewart

Reprinted 1982

0-7710-9504-X

The Canadian Publishers
McClelland and Stewart Limited
25 Hollinger Road, Toronto

Manufactured in Canada by Webcom Limited

CONTENTS

INTRODUCTION

The purpose of this anthology is to represent as fully as possible the poetry of a strictly limited number of those Canadian poets writing in English whose work started to appear during the years between 1940 and 1960. As the restriction to a few poets and to a particular era may suggest, my model is an earlier book in the same series: Malcolm Ross's selection from four *Poets of the Confederation*.

The standard anthologies of A. J. M. Smith and Ralph Gustafson range over the widest possible stretch of Canadian poetic time. They also seem anxious to include as many poets as possible from each era covered. As a glance at their contents makes evident, in the twentieth century scarcely a year has gone by without giving birth to one Canadian poet (and often more) fit to be anthologized, sometimes with only two or three poems, once in a long while with five or six. Such anthologies do admirable justice to the fertility and variety of Canadian poetry as a whole; they do less than justice to the range of invention of the best of the individual poets themselves. Since it seems impossible to be just in both ways at the same time, this anthology is designed to represent only a few poets, but to represent them at length, and has left the many other Canadian poets who have also written interesting poems to collections of a different kind.

My first intention was to follow my model exactly, and produce something that might be called *Four Recent Canadian Poets*. But there is nothing necessarily sacrosanct about the number four (for anthologists anyway), and it soon turned into five: Earle Birney, Irving Layton, Margaret Avison, Raymond Souster, and James Reaney. These five all, whatever their dates of birth, emerged as poets during the 1940's, were well established before the end of the decade, and have continued to demonstrate or extend their talents, and to publish their poems, throughout the 1950's. Among those Canadian poets who have followed such a pattern, they form, in my opinion, the best possible group of five; not just because of their cumulative poetic virtues, but also because it is hard to imagine five poets so unlike one another. They form no overlapping school; they follow in no sequence; they are no less distinct than they are talented.

This group of five having been decided on, a few nagging doubts nevertheless remained. Not about the group chosen, but about the principles which determined where to begin choosing and where to stop. As one of the poets himself remarked to me, "What about Frank Scott and A. J. M. Smith and A. M. Klein? They were still writing a lot in the forties and they made their presence felt on the new poets too." For that matter, one of E. J. Pratt's best poems, "The Truant," first appeared in 1942, not to mention *Towards the Last Spike*, ten years later. But such poets (one might add Dorothy Livesay to their number), despite their continued productivity, and despite the reluctance of publishers to collect their work into books before 1940, first made their mark in the twenties and belong in the anthology of an earlier poetic generation. What is more, if elder statesmen were to be included, they would deserve the same thorough treatment as their successors, and the anthology simply could not bear the weight.

So much for doubts about where to begin. What about where to stop? Much of the excitement in Canadian poetry of the fifties came from new poets unknown to the war generation, poets whose output is, as yet, comparatively restricted and could therefore with some justice be represented on a small scale. To include a further group of five poets might allow me to give a truer sense of the poetic life of the second decade and at the same time would not make necessary by its bulk any reduction in the thoroughness of representation essential for the five poets whose work spans the period as a whole. So, to the first five I have added comparatively brief selections from Leonard Cohen and Jay Macpherson, whose work first came into prominence in the mid-fifties, and from Alden Nowlan and Kenneth McRobbie, who were hardly known at all until about 1958. As a final choice for brief representation, making the total number ten, I have included, however, not a young poet near the beginning of his career, but an important older one who stopped early and has published no poetry for nearly ten years : P. K. Page, ninety per cent of whose work belongs to the forties, although much of it remained uncollected until 1954.

This anthology, then, aims at presenting a few individual poets in depth, but also at allowing some new voices to be heard as the two decades draw to a close. I hope that instead of being a mere compromise it succeeds equally well in doing both.

MILTON WILSON
Trinity College,
University of Toronto.

PART 1

EARLE

BIRNEY

Born in 1904 at Calgary, Earle Birney's early years were
spent in Alberta (mainly at Banff) and British Columbia
(Creston, in the Kootenays). He worked for two years at
assorted jobs before attending the University of British
Columbia. After graduation in 1926, he continued his English
studies at the University of Toronto, where a thesis on
"Chaucer's Irony" finally earned him a PH.D. and a position
in the English Department at University College in 1936.
His years as a graduate student were financed by a variety of
fellowships and teaching jobs, many of them in American
universities (California and Utah). His academic career was
interrupted both by the war, from which he emerged as a
major after serving for over three years as a Personnel
Selection Officer, and by a brief spell as Supervisor of Foreign
Language Broadcasts to Europe for the CBC. Since 1946 he
has been Professor of English at UBC and is now Chairman
of the newly formed Department of Writing.

No doubt partly from the competition of other preoccupations in the thirties, Birney's poetic career began late. His small output before 1940 is negligible, the obvious exception being "Slug in Woods," first printed in a *Canadian Forum* of 1937. Birney was the *Forum*'s literary editor from 1936 to 1942, in which year he left for the wars and published his widely acclaimed first book, *David and Other Poems* (The Ryerson Press). After the war Ryerson published two more collections, which mixed new and old work: *Now Is Time* (1945) and *The Strait of Anian* (1948). His fondness for Canadian topics and settings pleased those who looked for a poetry which would explain the country to itself, while his "virtuosity of language" earned the praise of those who looked for more specifically poetic virtues. The virtuosity was unmistakable (some reviewers even invoked Joyce) in the radio play on the "Proposed Damnation of Vancouver" which gave its title to *Trial of a City and Other Verse* (Ryerson, 1952). In the mid-fifties Birney printed few poems, but the years since 1958 have been among his most productive. *Ice Cod Bell or Stone* (McClelland and Stewart Limited) appeared in 1962 and *Near False Creek Mouth* in 1964. Birney has become something of a world traveller, and exotic settings are more common than Canadian in his recent work. He has published two novels, *Turvey* in 1949, and *Down the Long Table* in 1955.

❖

Slug in Woods

For eyes he waves greentipped
taut horns of slime.   They dipped,
hours back, across a reef,
a salmonberry leaf.

Then strained to grope past fin
of spruce. Now eyes suck in
as through the hemlock butts
of his day's ledge there cuts
a vixen chipmunk. Stilled
is he – green mucus chilled,
or blotched and soapy stone,
pinguid in moss, alone.
Hours on, he will resume
his silver scrawl, illume
his palimpsest, emboss
his diver's line across
that waving green illim-
itable seafloor. Slim
young jay his sudden shark;
the wrecks he skirts are dark
and fungussed firlogs, whom
spirea sprays emplume,
encoral. Dew his shell,
while mounting boles foretell
of isles in dappled air
fathoms above his care.
Azygous muted life,
himself his viscid wife,
foodward he noses cold beneath his sea.
So spends a summer's jasper century.

❖

World Winter

Sun
proud Bessemer   peltwarmer beauty
these winters yoke us   We scan sky for you
The dun droppings blur   we drown in snow
Is this tarnished chimneyplug   in a tenantless room
this sucked wafer   white simpleton
you?

Not
chiefly the months   mould you heartcharmer
to scant hammerdent   on hardiron sky
not alone latitude   to lodgers on this
your slantwhirling lackey   lifecrusted satellite
this your one wrynecked   woedealing
world

❖

Vancouver Lights

About me the night, moonless, wimples the mountains,
wraps ocean, land, air, and mounting
sucks at the stars. The city, throbbing below,
webs the sable peninsula. Streaming, the golden
strands overleap the seajet, by bridge and buoy
vault the shears of the inlet, climb the woods
toward me, falter and halt. Across to the firefly
haze of a ship on the gulf's erased horizon
roll the lambent spokes of a restless lighthouse.

Now through the feckless years we have come to the time
when to look on this quilt of lamps is a troubling delight.
Welling from Europe's bog, through Africa flowing
and Asia, drowning the lonely lumes on the oceans,
tiding up over Halifax, now to this winking
outpost comes flooding the primal ink.

On this mountain's brutish forehead with terror of space
I stir, of the changeless night and the stark ranges
of nothing, pulsing down from beyond and between
the fragile planets. We are a spark beleaguered
by darkness; this twinkle we make in a corner of emptiness,
how shall we utter our fear that the black Experimentress

will never in the range of her microscope find it? Our
    Phœbus
himself is a bubble that dries on Her slide, while the Nubian
wears for an evening's whim a necklace of nebulæ.

Yet we must speak, we the unique glowworms.
Out of the waters and rocks of our little world
we cunningly conjured these flames, hooped these sparks
by our will. From blankness and cold we fashioned stars
to our size, rulered with manplot the velvet chaos
and signalled Aldebaran. This must we say,
whoever may be to hear us, if murk devour,
and none weave again in gossamer :

                These rays were ours,
we made and unmade them. Not the shudder of continents
doused us, the moon's passion, nor crash of comets.
In the fathomless heat of our dwarfdom, our dream's
    combustion,
we contrived the power, the blast that snuffed us.
No one bound Prometheus. Himself he chained
and consumed his own bright liver. O stranger,
Plutonian, descendant, or beast in the stretching night –
there was light.

❧

Anglosaxon Street

Dawndrizzle ended,   dampness steams from
blotching brick and   blank plasterwaste.
Faded housepatterns,   hoary and finicky,
unfold stuttering,   stick like a phonograph.
Over the eaves and   over dank roofs
peep giraffetowers,   pasted planless
against greysky,   great dronecliffs
like cutouts for kids,   clipped in two dimensions.

Here is a ghetto   gotten for goyim
O with care denuded   of nigger and kike.
No coonsmell rankles,   reeks only cellarrot,
ottar of carexhaust,   catcorpse and cookinggrease.
Imperial hearts   heave in this haven.
Cracks across windows   are welded with slogans :
There'll Always Be An England   enhances geraniums,
and *V*'s for a *Victory*   vanquish the housefly.

Ho ! with climbing sun,   march the bleached beldames,
festooned with shoppingbags,   farded, flatarched,
bigthewed Saxonwives,   stepping over buttrivers,
waddling back to suckle   smallfry, wienerladen.

Hoy ! with sunslope,   shrieking over hydrants,
flood from learninghall   the lean fingerlings,
Nordic, nobblecheeked,   not all clean of nose,
leaping Commando-wise   into leprous lanes.

What ! after whistleblow,   spewed from wheelboat,
after daylong doughtiness,   dire handplay
in sewertrench or sandpit,   come Saxonthegns,
Junebrown Jutekings,   jawslack for meat.

Sit after supper   on smeared doorsteps,
not humbly swearing   hatedeeds on Huns,
profiteers, politicians,   pacifists, Jews.

Then by twobit magic   to muse in movie,
unlock picturehoard,   or lope to alehall,
soaking bleakly   in beer, skittleless.

Home again to hotbox   and humid husbandhood,
in slumbertrough adding   sleepily to Anglekin.
Alongside in lanenooks   carling and leman
caterwaul and clip,   careless of Saxonry,
with moonglow and haste   and a higher heartbeat.

Slumbers now slumtrack,   unstinks, cooling,
waiting brief for milkhind,   mornstar and worldrise.

David

David and I that summer cut trails on the Survey,
All week in the valley for wages, in air that was steeped
In the wail of mosquitoes, but over the sunalive weekends
We climbed, to get from the ruck of the camp, the surly

Poker, the wrangling, the snoring under the fetid
Tents, and because we had joy in our lengthening coltish
Muscles, and mountains for David were made to see over,
Stairs from the valleys and steps to the sun's retreats.

II

Our first was Mount Gleam. We hiked in the long afternoon
To a curling lake and lost the lure of the faceted
Cone in the swell of its sprawling shoulders. Past
The inlet we grilled our bacon, the strips festooned

On a poplar prong, in the hurrying slant of the sunset.
Then the two of us rolled in the blanket while round us the
    cold
Pines thrust at the stars. The dawn was a floating
Of mists till we reached to the slopes above timber, and won

To snow like fire in the sunlight. The peak was upthrust
Like a fist in a frozen ocean of rock that swirled
Into valleys the moon could be rolled in. Remotely
    unfurling
Eastward the alien prairie glittered. Down through the
    dusty

Skree on the west we descended, and David showed me
How to use the give of shale for giant incredible
Strides. I remember, before the larches' edge,
That I jumped a long green surf of juniper flowing

Away from the wind, and landed in gentian and saxifrage
Spilled on the moss. Then the darkening firs
And the sudden whirring of water that knifed down a
    fern-hidden
Cliff and splashed unseen into mist in the shadows.

III

One Sunday on Rampart's arête a rainsquall caught us,
And passed, and we clung by our blueing fingers and
    bootnails
An endless hour in the sun, not daring to move
Till the ice had steamed from the slate. And David taught me

How time on a knife-edge can pass with the guessing of
    fragments
Remembered from poets, the naming of strata beside one,
And matching of stories from schooldays. . . . We crawled
    astride
The peak to feast on the marching ranges flagged

By the fading shreds of the shattered stormcloud. Lingering
There it was David who spied to the south, remote,
And unmapped, a sunlit spire on Sawback, an overhang
Crooked like a talon. David named it the Finger.

That day we chanced on the skull and the splayed white ribs
Of a mountain goat underneath a cliff-face, caught
On a rock. Around were the silken feathers of hawks.
And that was the first I knew that a goat could slip.

IV

And then Inglismaldie. Now I remember only
The long ascent of the lonely valley, the live
Pine spirally scarred by lightning, the slicing pipe
Of invisible pika, and great prints, by the lowest

Snow, of a grizzly. There it was too that David
Taught me to read the scroll of coral in limestone
And the beetle-seal in the shale of ghostly trilobites,
Letters delivered to man from the Cambrian waves.

V

On Sundance we tried from the col and the going was hard.
The air howled from our feet to the smudged rocks
And the papery lake below. At an outthrust we balked
Till David clung with his left to a dint in the scarp,

Lobbed the iceaxe over the rocky lip,
Slipped from his holds and hung by the quivering pick,
Twisted his long legs up into space and kicked
To the crest. Then grinning, he reached with his freckled
    wrist

And drew me up after. We set a new time for that climb.
That day returning we found a robin gyrating
In grass, wing-broken. I caught it to tame but David
Took and killed it, and said, "Could you teach it to fly?"

VI

In August, the second attempt, we ascended The Fortress.
By the forks of the Spray we caught five trout and fried them
Over a balsam fire. The woods were alive
With the vaulting of mule-deer and drenched with clouds all
    the morning,

Till we burst at noon to the flashing and floating round
Of the peaks. Coming down we picked in our hats the bright
And sunhot raspberries, eating them under a mighty
Spruce, while a marten moving like quicksilver scouted us.

VII

But always we talked of the Finger on Sawback, unknown
And hooked, till the first afternoon in September we slogged
Through the musky woods, past a swamp that quivered with
    frog-song,
And camped by a bottle-green lake. But under the cold

Breath of the glacier sleep would not come, the moonlight
Etching the Finger. We rose and trod past the feathery
Larch, while the stars went out, and the quiet heather
Flushed, and the skyline pulsed with the surging bloom

Of incredible dawn in the Rockies. David spotted
Bighorns across the moraine and sent them leaping
With yodels the ramparts redoubled and rolled to the peaks,
And the peaks to the sun. The ice in the morning thaw

Was a gurgling world of crystal and cold blue chasms,
And seracs that shone like frozen saltgreen waves.
At the base of the Finger we tried once and failed. Then
     David
Edged to the west and discovered the chimney; the last

Hundred feet we fought the rock and shouldered and kneed
Our way for an hour and made it. Unroping we formed
A cairn on the rotting tip. Then I turned to look north
At the glistening wedge of giant Assiniboine, heedless

Of handhold. And one foot gave. I swayed and shouted.
David turned sharp and reached out his arm and steadied me,
Turning again with a grin and his lips ready
To jest. But the strain crumbled his foothold. Without

A gasp he was gone. I froze to the sound of grating
Edge-nails and fingers, the slither of stones, the lone
Second of silence, the nightmare thud. Then only
The wind and the muted beat of unknowing cascades.

VIII

Somehow I worked down the fifty impossible feet
To the ledge, calling and getting no answer but echoes
Released in the cirque, and trying not to reflect
What an answer would mean. He lay still, with his lean

Young face upturned and strangely unmarred, but his legs
Splayed beneath him, beside the final drop,
Six hundred feet sheer to the ice. My throat stopped
When I reached him, for he was alive. He opened his grey

Straight eyes and brokenly murmured "over . . . over."
And I, feeling beneath him a cruel fang
Of the ledge thrust in his back, but not understanding,
Mumbled stupidly, "Best not to move," and spoke

Of his pain. But he said, "I can't move. . . . If only I felt
Some pain." Then my shame stung the tears to my eyes
As I crouched, and I cursed myself, but he cried,
Louder, "No, Bobbie! Don't ever blame yourself.

I didn't test my foothold." He shut the lids
Of his eyes to the stare of the sky, while I moistened his lips
From our water flask and tearing my shirt into strips
I swabbed the shredded hands. But the blood slid

From his side and stained the stone and the thirsting lichens,
And yet I dared not lift him up from the gore
Of the rock. Then he whispered, "Bob, I want to go over!"
This time I knew what he meant and I grasped for a lie

And said, "I'll be back here by midnight with ropes
And men from the camp and we'll cradle you out." But I
    knew
That the day and the night must pass and the cold dews
Of another morning before such men unknowing

The ways of mountains could win to the chimney's top.
And then, how long? And he knew . . . and the hell of hours
After that, if he lived till we came, roping him out.
But I curled beside him and whispered, "The bleeding will
    stop.

You can last." He said only, "Perhaps. . . . For what? A
    wheelchair,
Bob?" His eyes brightening with fever upbraided me.
I could not look at him more and said, "Then I'll stay
With you." But he did not speak, for the clouding fever.

I lay dazed and stared at the long valley,
The glistening hair of a creek on the rug stretched
By the firs, while the sun leaned round and flooded the ledge,
The moss, and David still as a broken doll.

I hunched to my knees to leave, but he called and his voice
Now was sharpened with fear. "For Christ's sake push me
     over!
If I could move. . . . Or die. . . ." The sweat ran from his
     forehead,
But only his eyes moved. A hawk was buoying

Blackly its wings over the wrinkled ice.
The purr of a waterfall rose and sank with the wind.
Above us climbed the last joint of the Finger
Beckoning bleakly the wide indifferent sky.

Even then in the sun it grew cold lying there. . . . And I knew
He had tested his holds. It was I who had not. . . . I looked
At the blood on the ledge, and the far valley. I looked
At last in his eyes. He breathed, "I'd do it for you, Bob."

IX

I will not remember how nor why I could twist
Up the wind-devilled peak, and down through the chimney's
     empty
Horror, and over the traverse alone. I remember
Only the pounding fear I would stumble on It

When I came to the grave-cold maw of the bergschrund . . .
     reeling
Over the sun-cankered snowbridge, shying the caves
In the névé . . . the fear, and the need to make sure It was
     there
On the ice, the running and falling and running, leaping

Of gaping greenthroated crevasses, alone and pursued
By the Finger's lengthening shadow. At last through the
    fanged
And blinding seracs I slid to the milky wrangling
Falls at the glacier's snout, through the rocks piled huge

On the humped moraine, and into the spectral larches,
Alone. By the glooming lake I sank and chilled
My mouth but I could not rest and stumbled still
To the valley, losing my way in the ragged marsh.

I was glad of the mire that covered the stains, on my ripped
Boots, of his blood, but panic was on me, the reek
Of the bog, the purple glimmer of toadstools obscene
In the twilight. I staggered clear to a fire waste, tripped

And fell with a shriek on my shoulder. It somehow eased
My heart to know I was hurt, but I did not faint
And I could not stop while over me hung the range
Of the Sawback. In blackness I searched for the trail by the
    creek

And found it. . . . My feet squelched a slug and horror
Rose again in my nostrils. I hurled myself
Down the path. In the woods behind some animal yelped.
Then I saw the glimmer of tents and babbled my story.

I said that he fell straight to the ice where they found him,
And none but the sun and incurious clouds have lingered
Around the marks of that day on the ledge of the Finger,
That day, the last of my youth, on the last of our mountains.

Mappemounde

Not not this old   whalehall can whelm us
shiptamed gullgraced   soft to our glidings
Harrows that mere more   which squares our map
See in its north   where scribe has marked *mermen*
shore-sneakers who croon   to the seafarer's girl
next year's gleewords   East and west *nadders*
flamefanged bale-twisters   their breath dries up tears
chars in the breast-hoard   the brave picture-faces
Southward *Cetegrande*   that sly beast who sucks in
with whirlwind also   the wanderer's pledges
That sea is hight Time   it hems all hearts' landtrace
Men say the redeless   reaching its bounds
topple in maelstrom   tread back never
Adread in that mere   we drift to map's end

Hospital Ship "El Nil," Atlantic, 1945

❖

From the Hazel Bough

He met a lady
   on a lazy street
hazel eyes
   and little plush feet

her legs swam by
   like lovely trout
eyes were trees
   where boys leant out

hands in the dark and
   a river side
round breasts rising
   with the finger's tide

she was plump as a finch
   and live as a salmon
gay as silk and
   proud as a Brahmin

they winked when they met
   and laughed when they parted
never took time
   to be brokenhearted

but no man sees
   where the trout lie now
or what leans out
   from the hazel bough

❖

Ulysses

Make no mistake sailor the suitors are here
  and the clouds not yet quiet
Peace the bitchy Queen is back
  but a captive still on shelter diet
The girl of your heart has been knitting long
  the boy-friends have arms there may be a riot
Go canny of course but don't go wrong
  there's no guarantee of an epic ending
Your old dog Time prone on the dungpile
  offers the one last whick of his tail
while you amble by not daring to notice
  and the phony lords grow fat on your ale
Soldier keep your eye on the suitors
  have a talk with your son and the old hired man
but the bow is yours and you must bend it
  or you'll never finish what Homer began

Bushed

He invented a rainbow but lightning struck it
shattered it into the lake-lap of a mountain
so big his mind slowed when he looked at it

Yet he built a shack on the shore
learned to roast porcupine belly and
wore the quills on his hatband.

At first he was out with the dawn
whether it yellowed bright as wood-columbine
or was only a fuzzed moth in a flannel of storm
But he found the mountain was clearly alive
sent messages whizzing down every hot morning
boomed proclamations at noon and spread out
a white guard of goat
before falling asleep on its feet at sundown

When he tried his eyes on the lake, ospreys
would fall like valkyries
choosing the cut-throat
He took then to waiting
till the night smoke rose from the boil of the sunset

But the moon carved unknown totems
out of the lakeshore
owls in the beardusky woods derided him
moosehorned cedars circled his swamps and tossed
their antlers up to the stars
Then he knew though the mountain slept, the winds
were shaping its peak to an arrowhead
poised

But by now he could only
bar himself in and wait
for the great flint to come singing into his heart

Biography

At ten the years made tracks
plumped and sprung with pine-needles

Gaining height, overlooked
rock balanced on ridges
swords of snow in cliffside

Twenty he lay by the lake
the bright unpredictable book
gracefully bound in green
and riffled its pages for rainbow

Life was a pup-tent, ptarmigan
chased along simmering slopes
bannocks and bacon
Only the night-mists died at dawn

By thirty he trudged above timber
peered over ice at the peaks

As they swung slowly around him
the veins of bald glaciers blackened,
white pulses of waterfalls
beat in the bare rockflesh

Before him at forty
a nunatak stood like a sundial
swiftly marked time in the snow

Later a lancet of rime
hissed from the heave of the massif
a shrill wind shouldered him
and he turned

But tried without might
had lost the lake or his nerve
forgot all the trail-forks
knew at the end only
the ice knuckling his eyes

St Valentine Is Past

("St Valentine is past; begin these wood-birds
but to couple now?"—*A Midsummer Night's Dream*.)

When Theseus wheels his high deaf back
   hallooing toward the boar
they turn like teal to summer sea
   beat wordless to their shore

She walks then like a waterfall
   like all a water failing
and she is subtle as her spray
   below the sunlight paling

while he is rooted rock she strikes
   to foam a loud cascade
that drowns the jeering gullish wings
   far crashings in the glade

No more while lizard minutes sleep
   around a cactus land
they'll blow their longings out like spores
   that never grass the sand

No longer time's a cloud of cliffs
   unechoed by her Nile
he'll hide no more from suns that may
   elsewhere break out her smile

Daylong they watch their sky forget
   each old crow's winging shadow
"O we will build a dam of love
   and dapple all the meadow"

And yet and yet a failing rod
   strikes only dust from rock
while all the tune and time they breathe
   is never kept in talk

Now water sky and rock are gone
   the huddled woodbirds back
and hot upon the throbbing boar
   comes Theseus with his pack

❖

Can. Lit.

Since we had always sky about,
when we had eagles they flew out
leaving no shadow bigger than wren's
to trouble our most æromantic hens.
Too busy bridging loneliness to be alone
we hacked in ties what Emily etched in bone.
We French, we English, never lost our civil war,
endure it still, a bloodless civil bore;
no wounded lying about, no Whitman wanted.
It's only by our lack of ghosts we're haunted.

❖

Ellesmereland

Explorers say that harebells rise
from the cracks of Ellesmereland
and cod swim fat beneath the ice
that grinds its meagre sands
No man is settled on that coast
The harebells are alone
Nor is there talk of making man
from ice cod bell or stone

A Walk in Kyoto

All week, the maid tells me, bowing
her doll's body at my mat, is Boys' Day.
Also please Man's Day, and gravely
bends deeper. The magnolia sprig in my alcove,
is it male? The ancient discretions of Zen were not shaped
for my phallic western eye. There is so much discretion
in this small bowed body of an empire –
the wild hair of waterfalls combed straight
in the ricefields, the inn-maid retreating
with the face of a shut flower – I stand hunched
and clueless like a castaway in the shoals of my room.

When I slide my parchment door to stalk awkward
through Lilliput gardens framed and untouchable
as watercolours, the streets look much the same :
the Men are being pulled past on the strings of their engines,
the legs of the Boys are revolved by a thousand pedals,
and all the faces as taut and unfestive as Moscow's
or Toronto's or mine.

Lord Buddha help us all there is vigour enough
in these islands and in all islands reefed and resounding
with cities. But the pitch is high as the ping
of cicadas, those small strained motors concealed
in the propped pines by the dying river, and only
male as the stretched falsetto of actors mincing
the women's roles in *kabuki*, or female only
as the lost heroes womanized in the Ladies' Opera.
Where in these alleys jammed with competing waves
of signs in two tongues and three scripts
can the simple song of a man be heard?

By the shoguns' palace, the Important Cultural Property
stripped for tiptoeing schoolgirls, I stare at the staring
penned carp that flail on each other's backs

to the shrunk pool's edge for the crumb this non-fish
tossed. Is this the Day's one parable?
Or under that peeling pagoda the five hundred tons
of hermaphrodite Word?

At the inn I prepare to surrender again my defeated
shoes to the bending maid. But suddenly the closed
lotus opens to a smile and she points
over my shoulder, above the sagging tiles, to where
tall in the bare sky and huge as Gulliver
a carp is rising golden and fighting
thrusting its paper body up from the fist
of a small boy on an empty roof higher
and higher into the endless winds of the world.

Mammorial Stunzas for Aimee Simple McFarcin

Ah but I saw her ascend up in the assendupping breeze

There was a cloudfall of Kewpids
their glostening buttums twankling
in the gaggle-eyed and deleted air

We had snuk away from the Stemple
the whoopaluyah mongrelation
pigging their dolourbills to the kliegbright wires

We wondered at dawn into the cocacold desert
where bitchy torsouls of cacteyes prinked at us

Then soddenly she was gone with cupidities
vamoostered
with pink angelinoes

O mamomma we never forguess you
and your bag blue sheikel-getting ayes
loused, lost from all hallow Hollowood O

Aimee Aimee Tekel Upharsin

❖

Sinaloa

Si, señor, is halligators here, your guidebook say it,
si, jaguar in the montanas, maybe helephants, quien sabe?
You like, those palm trees in the sunset? Certamente very
    nice,
it happen each night in the guide tourista.
But who the hell eat jaguar, halligator, you heat them?
Mira my fren, wat this town need is muy big breakwater –
    I like take hax to them jeezly palmas.

So you want buy machete? Por favor, I give you
sousand machete you give me one grand bulldozer, hey?
Wat this country is lack, señor, is real good goosin,
is need pinehapple shove hup her bottom
(sure, sure, is bella all those water-ayacints)
is need drains for sugarcane in them pittoresca swamps –
    and shoot all them anarquista egrets.

Hokay, you like bugambilla, ow you say, flower-hung cliffs?
Is how old, the Fort? Is Colhuan, muy viejo, before Moses,
    no?
Is for you, señor, take em away, send us helevator for weat.
It like me to see all them fine boxcar stuff full rice,
sugar, flax, all rollin down to those palmstudded ports
were Cortez and all that crap (you heat history?) –
    and bugger the pink flamingos.

Amigo, we make you present all them two-weel hoxcart,
you send em Quebec, were my brudder was learn to be padre,
we take ditchdiggers, tractors, Massey-Arris yes?
Sinalóa want ten sousand mile irrigation canals,
absolutamente. Is fun all that organ-cactus fence?
Is for the birds, señor; is more better barbwire, verdad? –
   and chingar those cute little burros.

Sin argumento, my fren, is a beautiful music,
all them birds. Pero, wy you no like to ear combos,
refrigerator trucks? Is wonderful on straight new ighway,
jampack with melons, peppers, bananas, tomatoes, si, si . . .
Chirrimoyas? Mangos? You like! Is for Indios, solamente,
is bruise, no can ship, is no bueno, believe me, señor –
   and defecar on those goddam guidebook.

Six-Sided Square: Actopan

Do tell me what the ordinary Mex
Madam, there is a plaza in Actopan
where ladies very usual beside most rigid hexagrams
of chili peppers squat this moment
and in Ottomi gutturals not in Spanish lexicons
gossip while they scratch there in the open

But arent there towns in Mexico more av – ? Dear madam,
Actopan is a town more average than mean.
You may approach it on a sound macadam,
yet prone upon the plaza's cobbles will be seen
a brace of ancients, since no edict has forbad them,
under separate sarapes in a common pulque dream –

But someone has to work to make a – Lady,
those ladies work at selling hexametric chili,
and all their husbands, where the zocalo is shady,
routinely spin in silent willynilly
lariats from cactus muscles; as they braid they
hear their normal sons in crimson shorts go shrilly,

bouncing an oval basketball about the square –
You mean that all the younger gener – ?
I mean this is a saint's day, nothing rare,
a median saint, a medium celebration,
while pigeon-walking down the plaza stair
on tiny heels, from hexahemeric concentration

within the pyramidal church some architect
of Cortez built to tame her antecedents –
You mean that Mexico forgets her histor – ? Madam, I suspect
that patterns more complex must have precedence :
she yearns to croon in Harlem dialect
while still her priest to Xipe prays for intercedence.

Actópans all are rounded with the ordinary,
and sexed
much as they feel. *You mean –*
they are more hex-
agon and more extraordinary
than even you, dear lady, or than Egypt's queens

El Greco: Espolio

The carpenter is intent on the pressure of his hand
on the awl, and the trick of pinpointing his strength
through the awl to the wood, which is tough.
He has no effort to spare for despoilings
nor to worry if he'll be cut in on the dice.
His skill is vital to the scene, and the safety of the state.
Anyone can perform the indignities; it is his hard arms
and craft that hold the eyes of the convict's women.
There is the problem of getting the holes straight
(in the middle of this shoving crowd)
and deep enough to hold the spikes
after they've sunk through those soft feet
and wrists waiting behind him.

The carpenter isnt aware that one of the hands
is held in a curious beseechment over him –
but what is besought, forgiveness or blessing? –
nor if he saw would he take the time to be puzzled.
Criminals come in all sorts, as anyone knows who makes
     crosses,
are as mad or sane as those who decide on their killings.
Our one at least has been quiet so far
though they say he has talked himself into this trouble –
a carpenter's son who got notions of preaching.
Well here's a carpenter's son who'll have carpenter's sons,
God willing, and build what's wanted, temples or tables,
mangers or crosses, and shape them decently,
working alone in that firm and profound abstraction
which blots out the bawling of rag-snatchers.
To construct with hands, knee-weight, braced thigh,
keeps the back turned from death.
But it's too late now for the other carpenter's boy
to return to this peace before the nails are hammered.

The Bear on the Delhi Road

Unreal, tall as a myth
by the road the Himalayan bear
is beating the brilliant air
with his crooked arms.
About him two men, bare,
spindly as locusts, leap.
One pulls on a ring
in the great soft nose; his mate
flicks, flicks with a stick
up at the rolling eyes.

They have not led him here,
down from the fabulous hills
to this bald, alien plain
and the clamorous world, to kill
but simply to teach him to dance.

They are peaceful both, these spare
men of Kashmir, and the bear
alive is their living too.
If far on the Delhi way
around him galvanic they dance
it is merely to wear, wear
from his shaggy body the tranced
wish forever to stay
only an ambling bear
four-footed in berries.

It is no more joyous for them
in this hot dust to prance
out of reach of the praying claws
sharpened to paw for ants
in the shadows of deodars.
It is not easy to free
myth from reality
or rear this fellow up
to lurch, lurch with them
in the tranced dancing of men.

For George Lamming

To you
        I can risk words about this

Mastering them   you know
            they are dull
                servants
who say less
        and worse
                than we feel

That party above Kingston Town
        we stood   five (six?)   couples
linked singing
        more than rum happy

I was giddy
        from sudden friendship
        wanted   undeserved

        black tulip faces

        self swaying forgotten

        laughter in dance

Suddenly on a wall mirror
        my face assaulted me
stunned to see itself
        like a white snail
        in the supple dark flowers

Always now
    I move grateful
        to all of you
who let me walk thoughtless
        and unchallenged in the gardens
            in the castles
                of your skins

Plaza del Inquisición

A spider's body
limp and hairy
appeared at the bottom of my coffee

The waiter being Castilian
said passionately nothing
and why indeed should apologies
be made to me

It was I who was looking in
at the spider
It might be years
before I slipped and drowned
in Somebody Else's cup

IRVING LAYTON

A year after his birth in Roumania in 1912, Irving Layton moved to Montreal and has spent most of his time there ever since. He has a B.SC in Agriculture from Macdonald College (1939) and an MA in Economics and Political Science from McGill (1946). He published two books of poetry in the forties and an average of about one book a year since then. His stories are collected in *The Swinging Flesh* (1961) and *Collected Poems* (1965), both published by McClelland and Stewart Limited.

The new poets of wartime Montreal thrived on controversy, with John Sutherland's *First Statement* and Patrick Anderson's *Preview* as their chief periodical instruments, and established poets A. M. Klein and F. R. Scott as their mentors. Layton's poetry emerged out of this milieu and, when Sutherland founded *Northern Review* in 1945, he was one of its most active editors and contributors. The best of his early poetry is collected in *The Black Huntsman* (1951), but by this time he had broken with Sutherland, whose views had changed radically since 1945. Outside of colleagues, early Layton had few to praise him. *In the Midst of My Fever* (1954) marks a turning point in his poetic reputation and, for some readers at least, in his poetic development as well. His comprehensive collections *The Improved Binoculars* (Jonathan Williams and Contact Press, 1956) and *A Red Carpet for the Sun* (McClelland and Stewart Limited, 1959) were received with remarkable critical enthusiasm and widespread popularity, although dissenting voices have lately shown signs of revival.

Teaching is almost as strong a vocation for Layton as writing poems. His talent for forthright public controversy has made his views known to many who have never read his books. He has taught the reading and writing of poetry to students in Montreal secondary schools, and at Sir George Williams University, since the early fifties, and his influence on young poets has extended well beyond Montreal.

❖

The Swimmer

The afternoon foreclosing, see
The swimmer plunges from his raft,
Opening the spray corollas by his act of war –
The snake heads strike
Quickly and are silent.

Emerging see how for a moment
A brown weed with marvellous bulbs,
He lies imminent upon the water
While light and sound come with a sharp passion
From the gonad sea around the Poles
And break in bright cockle-shells about his ears.

He dives, floats, goes under like a thief
Where his blood sings to the tiger shadows
In the scentless greenery that leads him home,
A male salmon down fretted stairways
Through underwater slums . . .

Stunned by the memory of lost gills
He frames gestures of self-absorption
Upon the skull-like beach;
Observes with instigated eyes
The sun that empties itself upon the water,
And the last wave romping in
To throw its boyhood on the marble sand.

❖

Mont Roliand

Pitiless towards men, I am filled with pity
For the impractical trees climbing the exhausted hillside;
Sparse, dull, with blue uneven spaces between them,
They're like the beard of an uncombed tolerant monk,
        Or a Tolstoyan disciple, circa 1890.

Below these, a straggler, a tree with such enormous boughs
It might have remembered Absalom, who dead,
Put by the aping of his father's majesty;
And one lone cedar, a sycophant, stunted,
        A buffoon with sick dreams.

While all around me, as for a favoured intruder,
There's an immense silence made for primeval birds
Or a thought to rise like a great cloud out of a crater,
A silence contained by valleys,
        Gardes Civiles in green capes.

Nevertheless the Lilliput train trivializes
The tolerant monk, the trees, and this whirlpool of silence,
Though it fling over its side like a capitalist's bequest
A memorial row
      Of blossoming cherry trees.

And the highway which seen from my window seems
A suture in the flesh of a venerable patrician,
In the distance falls like a lariat on the green necks
Of the untamed hills, that raise like wild horses
      Their dignified, astonished heads.

❖

Vexata Quaestio

I fixing my eyes upon a tree
Maccabean among the dwarfed
      Stalks of summer
Listened for ship's sound and birdsong
And felt the bites of insects
      Expiring in my arms' hairs.

And there among the green prayerful birds
Among the corn I heard
      The chaffering blades:
"You are no flydung on cherry blossoms,
Among two-legged lice
      You have the gift of praise.

Give your stripped body to the sun
Your sex to any skilled
      And pretty damsel;
From the bonfire
Of your guilts make
      A blazing Greek sun."

Then the wind which all day
Had run regattas through the fields
    Grew chill, became
A tree-dismantling wind;

The sun went down
    And called my brown skin in.

❖

Cemetery in August

In August, white butterflies
Engage twig and rock;
Love-sheaths bloom in convenient fissures
On a desiccated stalk;
The generation of Time brings
Rind, shell, delicate wings

And mourners. Amidst this
Summer's babble of small noises
They weep, or interject
Their resentful human voices;
At timely intervals
I am aware of funerals.

And these iambic stones
Honouring who-knows-what bones
Seem in the amber sunlight
Patient and confounded
Like men enduring an epoch
Or one bemused by proofs of God.

To the Girls of My
Graduating Class

Wanting for their young limbs praise,
Their thighs, hips, and saintly breasts,
    They grow from awkwardness to delight,
Their mouths made perfect with the air
    About them and the sweet rage in the blood,
    The delicate trouble in their veins.

Intolerant as happiness, suddenly
They'll dart like bewildered birds;
    For there's no mercy in that bugler Time
That excites against their virginity
    The massed infantry of days, nor in the tendrils
    Greening on their enchanted battlements.

Golda, Fruma, Dinnie, Elinor,
My saintly wantons, passionate nuns;
    O light-footed daughters, your unopened
Brittle beauty troubles an aging man
    Who hobbles after you a little way
    Fierce and ridiculous.

❖

Composition in Late Spring

When Love ensnares my mind unbidden
        I am lost in the usual way
On a crowded street or avenue
Where I am lord of all the marquees,
And the traffic cop moving his lips
        Like a poet composing
Whistles a discovery of sparrows
About my head.

My mind, full of goats and pirates
                And simpler than a boy's,
I walk through a forest of white arms
That embrace me like window-shoppers;
Friends praise me like a Turkish delight
                Or a new kind of suspender
And children love me
Like a story.

Conscience more flat than cardboard
                Over the gap in a sole,
I avoid the fanatic whose subway
Collapsed in his brain;
There's a sinking, but the madonna
                Who clings to my hairlock
Is saved : on shore the damned ones
Applaud with the vigour of bees.

The sparrows' golden plummeting
                From fearful rooftop
Shows the flesh dying into sunshine.
Fled to the green suburbs, Death
Lies scared to death under a heap of bones.
                Beauty buds from mire
And I, a singer in season, observe
Death is a name for beauty not in use.

No one is more happy, none can do more tricks.
                The sun melts like butter
Over my sweetcorn thoughts;
And, at last, both famous and good
I'm a Doge, a dog
                At the end of a terrace
Where poems like angels like flakes of powder
Quaver above my prickling skin.

The Birth of Tragedy

And me happiest when I compose poems.
        Love, power, the huzza of battle
        are something, are much;
yet a poem includes them like a pool
        water and reflection.
In me, nature's divided things –
        tree, mould on tree –
        have their fruition;
I am their core. Let them swap,
bandy, like a flame swerve
I am their mouth; as a mouth I serve.

And I observe how the sensual moths
        big with odour and sunshine
        dart into the perilous shrubbery;
or drop their visiting shadows
        upon the garden I one year made
of flowering stone to be a footstool
        for the perfect gods :
        who, friends to the ascending orders,
sustain all passionate meditations
and call down pardons
for the insurgent blood.

A quiet madman, never far from tears,
        I lie like a slain thing
        under the green air the trees
inhabit, or rest upon a chair
        towards which the inflammable air
tumbles on many robins' wings;
        noting how seasonably
        leaf and blossom uncurl
and living things arrange their death,
while someone from afar off
blows birthday candles for the world.

Misunderstanding

I placed
my hand
upon
her thigh.

By the way
she moved
away
I could see
her devotion
to literature
was not
perfect.

❖

Look,
the Lambs Are All
Around Us!

Your figure, love,
curves itself
into a man's memory;
or to put it the way
a junior prof
at Mount Allison might,
Helen with her thick
absconding limbs
about the waist
of Paris
did no better.

Hell, my back's sunburnt
from so much love-making
in the open air.
The Primate (somebody
made a monkey of him)
and the Sanhedrin
(long on the beard, short
on the brain)
send envoys to say
they don't approve.
You never see them, love.
You toss me in the air
with such abandon,
they take to their heels and run.
I tell you
each kiss of yours
is like a blow on the head!

What luck, what luck to be loved
by the one girl
in this Presbyterian
country
who knows how to give
a man pleasure.

❖

The Cold Green Element

At the end of the garden walk
the wind and its satellite wait for me;
their meaning I will not know
        until I go there,
but the black-hatted undertaker

who, passing, saw my heart beating in the grass
is also going there. Hi, I tell him,
a great squall in the Pacific blew a dead poet
        out of the water,
who now hangs from the city's gates.

Crowds depart daily to see it, and return
with grimaces and incomprehension;
if its limbs twitched in the air
        they would sit at its feet
peeling their oranges.

And turning over I embrace like a lover
the trunk of a tree, one of those
for whom the lightning was too much
        and grew a brilliant
hunchback with a crown of leaves.

The ailments escaped from the labels
of medicine bottles are all fled to the wind;
I've seen myself lately in the eyes
        of old women,
spent streams mourning my manhood,

in whose old pupils the sun became
a bloodsmear on broad catalpa leaves
and hanging from ancient twigs,
        my murdered selves
sparked the air like the muted collisions

of fruit. A black dog howls down my blood,
a black dog with yellow eyes;
he too by someone's inadvertence
        saw the bloodsmear
on the broad catalpa leaves.

But the furies clear a path for me to the worm
who sang for an hour in the throat of a robin,
and misled by the cries of young boys
        I am again
a breathless swimmer in that cold green element.

Enemies

The young carpenter
        who works on his house
has no definition for me.

I am for him
        a book. A face in a book.
Finally a face.

The sunlight
        on the white paper
The sunlight on the easy

Summer chair
        is the same sunlight
which glints rosily

From his hammer.
        He is aware suddenly
of connections : I

Am embroiled
        in the echoing sound
of his implement

As it slides nails
        into the resistant wood
from which later, later

Coffins will emerge
        as if by some monstrous
parturition. Is it any wonder

He so mislikes me
        seeing his handiwork
robed in black ?

Seeing I shatter
        his artifact of space
with that which is

Forever dislodging
        the framework for
its own apprehension?

Over the wall
        of sound I see
his brutal grin of victory

Made incomplete
        by the white sunlit
paper I hold on my knee.

He has no metal
        gauge to take in
a man with a book

And yet his
        awkward shadow
falls on each page.

We are implicated,
        in each other's presence
by the sun, the third party

(Itself unimplicated)
        and only for a moment
reconciled to each other's

Necessary existence
        by the sight
of our neighbour's

Excited boy
        whom some God, I conjecture,
bounces for His joy.

As a beginning, the small bird
And the small twig will do; the green
Smudge across the windowpanes
And the gathering dark; the insects
Outside, hungry, harried, hopeful,
Clamouring. As a beginning,
The bottles of amber ale, or the vexed
Stillness in the pioneer room
When no one spoke.

Then say, these were the gifted
Actors whose egotism, not green
Nor lovely as that of towering trees,
Broke the silences in the forest
Like a bulldozer. Smith, a mild
Eighteenth century man, warm
And wanting praise, therefore not dead.
Frank Scott, proffering us the hard
Miracle of complexity
And humaneness, his face serpent
Benevolent.

And my proud friend,
Dudek, put out because the blades
Did not sufficiently applaud him
And the long-tailed thrashers ignored
His singing altogether.
A sad man. Rouault : Le Clown Blesse
And Currie, drained of sex, a blight.
And other, littler firtrees giving
Their gay needles to the breeze.

All of them coughing like minor
Poets; all of them building
To themselves tall monuments
Of remaindered verse; all of them

Apprehending more of goodness
And wisdom than they could practise;
All of them, in word and act,
Timesputtering, foaming white
Like sodium chloride on water.

And then add this : though not trees
Green and egotistical making
Somehow a forest of peace,
Nor a lake dropped like a stone
Into the stillness which thereafter
Reproves the intruder in liquid
Accents; though no unsullen harebells
But a congregation of sick egotists,
We shall endure, and they with us;
Our names told quietly across
These waters, having fixed this moment
In a phrase which these – trees, flowers, birds –
For all their self-assertion cannot do.

❖

Song for Naomi

Who is that in the tall grasses singing
By herself, near the water?
I can not see her
But can it be her
Than whom the grasses so tall
Are taller,
My daughter,
My lovely daughter?

Who is that in the tall grasses running
Beside her, near the water?
She can not see there
Time that pursued her
In the deep grasses so fast
And faster
And caught her,
My foolish daughter.

What is the wind in the fair grass saying
Like a verse, near the water?
Saviours that over
All things have power
Make Time himself grow kind
And kinder
That sought her,
My little daughter.

Who is that at the close of the summer
Near the deep lake? Who wrought her
Comely and slender?
Time but attends and befriends her
Than whom the grasses though tall
Are not taller,
My daughter,
My gentle daughter.

❖

Golfers

Like Sieur Montaigne's distinction
between virtue and innocence
what gets you is their unbewilderment

They come into the picture suddenly
like unfinished houses, gapes and planed wood,
dominating a landscape

And you see at a glance
among sportsmen they are the metaphysicians,
intent, untalkative, pursuing Unity

(What finally gets you is their chastity)

And that no theory of pessimism is complete
which altogether ignores them

❖

Maurer: Twin Heads

The one is reticent, carries himself well;
Is free in manner, yet unapproachable;
    He makes us think certain temperate days
Can put a chill between the shoulderblades.
He uses courtesy like a knife.

Listen : for all his careful fuss,
Will this cold one ever deceive us?
    Self-hating, he rivets a glittering wall:
Impairs it by a single pebble
And loves himself for that concession.

The other, seemingly his opposite, grabs friend
Or cousin with an elastic hand;
    Is, if anything, ridiculous
In his intemperance to please :
Yet is to sovereign eyes his brother's brother.

For by unloading favours on
Friend and unsuspecting cousin
    He subverts each with guilt and crawls
Happily at last among equals.
He loves himself for the moist confession.

The cold one coming slowly down;
His brother, on knees, the easier to climb,
    Meet upon a safe and velvet stair :
All footfalls deadened, here's
No father's tread, and no terror.

❖

Whatever Else
Poetry is Freedom

Whatever else poetry is freedom.
Forget the rhetoric, the trick of lying
All poets pick up sooner or later. From the river,
Rising like the thin voice of grey castratos – the mist;
Poplars and pines grow straight but oaks are gnarled;
Old codgers must speak of death, boys break windows;
Women lie honestly by their men at last.

And I who gave my Kate a blackened eye
Did to its vivid changing colours
Make up an incredible musical scale;
And now I balance on wooden stilts and dance
And thereby sing to the loftiest casements.
See how with polish I bow from the waist.
Space for these stilts ! More space or I fail !

And a crown I say for my buffoon's head.
Yet no more fool am I than King Canute,
Lord of our tribe, who scanned and scorned;
Who half-deceived, believed; and, poet, missed
The first white waves come nuzzling at his feet:
Then damned the courtiers and the foolish trial
With a most bewildering and unkingly jest.

It was the mist. It lies inside one like a destiny.
A real Jonah it lies rotting like a lung.
And I know myself undone who am a clown
And wear a wreath of mist for a crown;
Mist with the scent of dead apples,
Mist swirling from black oily waters at evening,
Mist from the fraternal graves of cemeteries.

It shall drive me to beg my food and at last
Hurl me broken I know and prostrate on the road;
Like a huge toad I saw, entire but dead,
That Time mordantly had blacked; O pressed
To the moist earth it pled for entry.
I shall be I say that stiff toad for sick with mist
And crazed I smell the odour of mortality.

And Time flames like a paraffin stove
And what it burns are the minutes I live.
At certain middays I have watched the cars
Bring me from afar their windshield suns;
What lay to my hand were blue fenders,
The suns extinguished, the drivers wearing sunglasses.
And it made me think I had touched a hearse.

So whatever else poetry is freedom. Let
Far off the impatient cadences reveal
A padding for my breathless stilts. Swivel,
O hero, in the fleshy groves, skin and glycerine,
And sing of lust, the sun's accompanying shadow
Like a vampire's wing, the stillness in dead feet –
Your stave brings resurrection, O aggrievèd king.

Berry Picking

Silently my wife walks on the still wet furze
Now darkgreen the leaves are full of metaphors
Now lit up is each tiny lamp of blueberry.
The white nails of rain have dropped and the sun is free.

And whether she bends or straightens to each bush
To find the children's laughter among the leaves
Her quiet hands seem to make the quiet summer hush –
Berries or children, patient she is with these.

I only vex and perplex her; madness, rage
Are endearing perhaps put down upon the page;
Even silence daylong and sullen can then
Enamour as restraint or classic discipline.

So I envy the berries she puts in her mouth,
The red and succulent juice that stains her lips;
I shall never taste that good to her, nor will they
Displease her with a thousand barbarous jests.

How they lie easily for her hand to take,
Part of the unoffending world that is hers;
Here beyond complexity she stands and stares
And leans her marvellous head as if for answers.

No more the easy soul my childish craft deceives
Nor the simpler one for whom yes is always yes;
No, now her voice comes to me from a far way off
Though her lips are redder than the raspberries.

Cain

Taking the air rifle from my son's hand,
I measured back five paces, the Hebrew
In me, narcissist, father of children,
Laid to rest. From there I took aim and fired.
The silent ball hit the frog's back an inch
Below the head. He jumped at the surprise
Of it, suddenly tickled or startled
(He must have thought) and leaped from the wet sand
Into the surrounding brown water. But
The ball had done its mischief. His next spring
Was a miserable flop, the thrust all gone
Out of his legs. He tried – like Bruce – again,
Throwing out his sensitive pianist's
Hands as a dwarf might or a helpless child.
His splash disturbed the quiet pondwater
And one old frog behind his weedy moat
Blinking, looking self-complacently on.
The lin's surface at once became closing
Eyelids and bubbles like notes of music
Liquid, luminous, dropping from the page
White, white-bearded, a rapid crescendo
Of inaudible sounds and a crones' whispering
Backstage among the reeds and bulrushes
As for an expiring Lear or Oedipus.

But Death makes us all look ridiculous.
Consider this frog (dog, hog, what you will)
Sprawling, his absurd corpse rocked by the tides
That his last vain spring had set in movement.
Like a retired oldster, I couldn't help sneer,
Living off the last of his insurance :
Billows – now crumbling – the premiums paid.
Absurd, how absurd. I wanted to kill
At the mockery of it, kill and kill
Again – the self-infatuate frog, dog, hog,
Anything with the stir of life in it,
Seeing the dead leaper, Chaplin-footed,

Rocked and cradled in this afternoon
Of tranquil water, reeds, and blazing sun,
The hole in his back clearly visible
And the torn skin a blob of shadow
Moving when the quiet poolwater moved.
O Egypt, marbled Greece, resplendent Rome,
Did you also finally perish from a small bore
In your back you could not scratch? And would
Your mouths open ghostily, gasping out
Among the murky reeds, the hidden frogs,
We climb with crushed spines toward the heavens?

When the next morning I came the same way
The frog was on his back, one delicate
Hand on his belly, and his white shirt front
Spotless. He looked as if he might have been
A comic; tapdancer apologizing
For a fall, or an Emcee, his wide grin
Coaxing a laugh from us for an aside
Or perhaps a joke we didn't quite hear.

❖

Family Portrait

That owner of duplexes
has enough gold to sink himself
on a battleship. His children,
two sons and a daughter, are variations
on the original gleam : that is,
    slobs with a college education.

Right now the four of them
are seated in the hotel's dining-room
munching watermelons.

With the assurance of money
in the bank
they spit out the black, cool, elliptical
melonseeds, and you can tell
the old man has rocks
but no culture : he spits,
    gives the noise away free.

The daughter however is embarrassed
(Second Year Arts, McGill) and sucks harder
to forget.

They're about as useless
as tits on a bull,
and I think :
"Thank heaven I'm not
 Jesus Christ –
 I don't have to love them."

❖

Côte des Neiges Cemetery

As if it were a faultless poem, the odour
Is both sensuous and intellectual,
And of faded onion peel its colour;
For here the wasting mausoleums brawl
With Time, heedless and mute; their voice
Kept down, polite yet querulous –
Assuredly courtesy must at last prevail.

Away from the markings of the poor
On slope and summit the statuary is vain
And senatorial (now the odour's
A high-pitched note, piercing the brain)
Where lying together are judge and barrister
And some whose busts look on a shrunk estate.

Persuade yourself it is a Warner set
Unreal and two-dimensional, a façade,
Though our mortal tongues are furred with death :
A ghost city where live autumn birds flit
And small squirrels dart from spray to spray
And this formal scene is a kind of poetry.

Especially the tomb of Moise Wong, alien
And quaint among French Catholic names
Or the drainage pipes inanimate and looped
You may conceive as monstrous worms.
Undying paradox ! Yet, love, look again :
Like an insinuation of leaves in snow

And sad, sad with surrender are the tablets
For the Chinese nuns; or, a blade between, the rows
Exact as alms, of les Sourdes et Muettes
And of les Aveugles : – and this, dear girl,
Is the family plot of Père Loisel and his wife
Whose jumbled loins in amorous sweat
Spawned these five neat graves in a semicircle.

Cat Dying in Autumn

I put the cat outside to die,
Laying her down
Into a rut of leaves
Cold and bloodsoaked;
Her moan
Coming now more quiet
And brief in October's economy
Till the jaws
Opened and shut on no sound.

Behind the wide pane
I watched the dying cat
Whose fur like a veil of air
The autumn wind stirred
Indifferently with the leaves;
Her form (or was it the wind?)
Still breathing –
A surprise of white.

And I was thinking
Of melting snow in spring
Or a strip of gauze
When a sparrow
Dropped down beside it
Leaning his clean beak
Into the hollow;
Then whirred away, his wings,
You may suppose, shuddering.

Letting me see
From my house
The twisted petal
That fell
Between the ruined paws
To hold or play with,
And the tight smile
Cats have for meeting death.

The Day Aviva Came to Paris

The day you came naked to Paris
The tourists returned home without their guidebooks,
The hunger in their cameras finally appeased.

Alone once more with their gargoyles, the Frenchmen
Marvelled at the imagination that had produced them
And once again invited terror into their apéritifs.
Death was no longer exiled to the cemeteries.

In their royal gardens where the fish die of old age,
They perused something else besides newspapers
– A volume perhaps by one of their famous writers.
They opened their hearts to let your tender smile defrost
        them;
Their livers filled with an unassuageable love of justice.
They became the atmosphere around them.

They learned to take money from Americans
Without a feeling of revulsion towards them;
And to think of themselves
As not excessively subtle or witty.
"Au diable with Voltaire," they muttered,
"Who was a national calamity.
Au diable with la République.
(A race of incurable petits bourgeois, the French
Are happiest under a horse under a man)
Au diable with la Monarchie!
We saw no goddesses during either folly;
Our bald-headed savants never had told us
Such a blaze of pubic hair anywhere existed."
And they ordered the grandson of Grandma Moses
To paint it large on the dome of le Sacré-Coeur.

My little one, as if under those painted skies
It was again 1848,
They leaped as one mad colossal Frenchman from their
        café Pernods

Shouting, "Vive l'Australienne!
Vive Layton who brought her among us!
Let us erect monuments of black porphyry to them!
Let us bury them in the Panthéon!"

(Pas si vite, messieurs; we are still alive)

And when, an undraped Jewish Venus,
You pointed to a child, a whole slum starving in her eyes,
Within earshot of the Tuileries,
The French who are crazy or catholic enough
To place, facing each other, two tableaux
– One for the Men of the Convention, and one puffing
        the Orators of the Restoration –
At once made a circle wide as the sky around you
While the Mayor of the 5th Arondissement
Addressed the milling millions of Frenchmen:

"See how shapely small her adorable ass is;
Of what an incredible pink rotundity each cheek.
A bas Merovingian and Valois!
A bas Charlemagne and Henri Quatre!
For all the adulations we have paid them
In our fabulous histoires
They cannot raise an erection between them. Ah,
For too long has the madness of love
Been explained to us by sensualists and curés.
A bas Stendhal! A bas Bossuet!

"Forever and forever, from this blazing hour
All Paris radiates from Aviva's nest of hair
– Delicate hatchery of profound delights –
From her ever-to-be-adored Arche de Triomphe!
All the languors of history
Take on meaning clear as a wineglass or the belch of an
        angel
Only if thought of as rushing
On the wings of a rhinoceros towards this absorbing event.

Voyeurs, voyez! The moisture of her delicate instep
Is a pool of love
Into which sheathed in candy paper
Anaesthetized politicians drop from the skies!"
(Word jugglery of course, my Sweet; but the French love it
– Mistake it in fact for poetry)

And the applaudissements and bravos
Bombinating along the Boulevard Saint-Germain
Made the poor docile Seine
Think our great Atlantic was upon it.
It overflowed with fright into the bookstalls
And sidewalk cafés.
Fifteen remaining Allemands with their cameras
Were flushed down the Rue Pigalle.

And when you were raised up
Into my hairy arms by the raving emotional crowds
Waving frenzied bottles of Beaujolais
And throwing the corks away ecstatically
(Not saving them!)
It was, my Love, my Darling,
As if someone had again ordered an advance
Upon the Bastille
Which we recalled joyously, face to face at last,
Had yielded after only a small token resistance.

❖

The Convertible

Her breath already smelled of whiskey.
She lit a cigarette
And pointed to a flask in the glove compartment.
Then our mouths met.

She placed her hand on my groin;
She hadn't bothered to remove her wedding ring.
Her eyes closed with a sigh.
I was ready for the gathering.

You, Dulla, may prefer maidenheads;
But give me the bored young wives of Hampstead
Whose husbands provide them with smart convertibles
And who are reasonably well-read.

❧

The Architect

I put my hand through a hedge;
    the leaves of the roadside shrubbery stirred,
scattering immense grains of countryside dust.

The forest behind me began to sneeze,
    and blew into the quiet noon air
thrushes, sparrows, and red-winged cardinals.

They fell at my feet like coloured snowflakes;
    from their tiny, beautiful bones
I raised a city where the first bird had fallen.

The mayor's wife, resembling Alice B. Toklas,
    donated her most attractive smile
to decorate the flagpole of the tallest building.

On clear nights even dwarfs can see her dentures
    outlined against the sky as if
to snap at the moon or a moon man descending.

From a nearby swamp I came to another forest
    while humming the first faint banknotes
that came into my head and thinking of means

To squeeze the silver from the moon and stars.
    When I put my hand through a hedge
the forest just held its breath and gulped.

No bird dropped. A toad suddenly leaped up
    and looked me straight in the eye;
he remained suspended in mid air until he fell.

Yet when I pulled back my eager hand
    my wrist was thick as a porcupine
and ugly with huge unshaven bristles.

The toothless wife of the mayor, however,
    will not let me amputate:
my queer arm, she says, is a civic acquisition.

Together when we walk arm-in-arm on Sherbrooke St.
    we make an intriguing pair;
tourists of all countries just stand and stare.

❖

The Wooden Spoon

If the sky is an inverted bowl,
Let us turn it over;
Before you have done counting my locks,
It will be filled with nectar.

Here is a wooden spoon, my Sweet.
If your thoughts are subtle
And innocent as your breasts
It will reach the sky.

My first pet
Shaved my favourite knoll
And covered it with a bourgeois smirk;
She ordered me to walk
Always ten paces ahead of my shadow
And carried the spoon's image on the sand
To measure the distance.

Using the wrong end of a parable
She began to erase the crescents
Of my fingernails.
I made her swallow them
And soon after she died in an asylum,
Asking the full moon to draw closer
Asking the sun
Why it wanted to go on living forever.

Another darling begged the wooden spoon
For stirring her own broths;
At last she digested a splinter.
It came out of her ear
A twig of jellied moths;
The sinister purity of their colour
Blinded her for seven whole days.
Then I made my getaway.

Petite Calan said the spoon
Was a sexual talisman
And kept it wrapped in a bloodstained brassière,
Praising its hermaphrodite economy.
At Victoria Bridge I broke it carefully
Over her yellow hair.
The pleasure-hating tugboats
Saw the body fall into the loose water
And screamed.

My other wives, reared by Carmelite nuns,
Had never seen a wooden spoon.

Nevertheless, child, do not be frightened.
I am no Bluebeard.
Murdered poems are what you will find
Behind that locked door, my dear.

❖

Whom I Write For

When reading me, I want you to feel
    as if I had ripped your skin off;
Or gouged out your eyes with my fingers;
Or scalped you, and afterwards burnt your hair
    in the staring sockets; having first filled them
with fluid from your son's lighter.
I want you to feel as if I had slammed
    your child's head against a spike;
And cut off your member and stuck it in your
    wife's mouth to smoke like a cigar.

For I do not write to improve your soul;
    or to make you feel better, or more humane;
Nor do I write to give you new emotions;
Or to make you proud to be able to experience them
    or to recognize them in others.
I leave that to the fraternity of lying poets
    – no prophets, but toadies and trained seals!
How much evil there is in the best of them
    as their envy and impotence flower into poems
And their anality into love of man, into virtue :
Especially when they tell you, sensitively,
    what it feels like to be a potato.

I write for the young man, demented,
   who dropped the bomb on Hiroshima;
I write for Nasser and Ben Gurion;
For Krushchev and President Kennedy;
   for the Defence Secretary
voted forty-six billions for the extirpation
   of humans everywhere.
I write for the Polish officers machine-gunned
   in the Katyn forest;
I write for the gassed, burnt, tortured,
   and humiliated everywhere;
I write for Castro and tse-Tung, the only poets
   I ever learned anything from;
I write for Adolph Eichmann, compliant clerk
   to that madman, the human race;
For his devoted wife and loyal son.

Give me words fierce and jagged enough
   to tear your skin like shrapnel;
Hot and searing enough to fuse
   the flesh off your blackened skeleton;
Words with the sound of crunching bones or bursting
      eyeballs;
   or a nose being smashed with a gun butt;
Words with the soft plash of intestines
   falling out of your belly;
Or cruel and sad as the thought which tells you "This is the
      end"
And you feel Time oozing out of your veins
   and yourself becoming one with the weightless dark.

A Tall Man Executes a Jig

for Malcolm Ross

I

So the man spread his blanket on the field
And watched the shafts of light between the tufts
And felt the sun push the grass towards him;
The noise he heard was that of whizzing flies,
The whistlings of some small imprudent birds,
And the ambiguous rumbles of cars
That made him look up at the sky, aware
Of the gnats that tilted against the wind
And in the sunlight turned to jigging motes.
Fruitflies he'd call them except there was no fruit
About, spoiling to hatch these glitterings,
These nervous dots for which the mind supplied
The closing sentences from Thucydides,
Or from Euclid having a savage nightmare.

II

Jig jig, jig jig. Like minuscule black links
Of a chain played with by some playful
Unapparent hand or the palpitant
Summer haze bored with the hour's stillness.
He felt the sting and tingle afterwards
Of those leaving their orthodox unrest,
Leaving their undulant excitation
To drop upon his sleeveless arm. The grass,
Even the wildflowers became black hairs
And himself a maddened speck among them.
Still the assaults of the small flies made him
Glad at last, until he saw purest joy
In their frantic jiggings under a hair,
So changed from those in the unrestraining air.

III

He stood up and felt himself enormous.
Felt as might Donatello over stone,
Or Plato, or as a man who has held
A loved and lovely woman in his arms

And feels his forehead touch the emptied sky
Where all antinomies flood into light.
Yet jig jig jig, the haloing black jots
Meshed with the wheeling fire of the sun :
Motion without meaning, disquietude
Without sense or purpose, ephemerides
That mottled the resting summer air till
'Gusts swept them from his sight like wisps of smoke.
Yet they returned, bringing a bee who, seeing
But a tall man, left him for a marigold.

IV

He doffed his aureole of gnats and moved
Out of the field as the sun sank down,
A dying god upon the blood-red hills.
Ambition, pride, the ecstasy of sex,
And all circumstance of delight and grief,
That blood upon the mountain's side, that flood
Washed into a clear incredible pool
Below the ruddied peaks that pierced the sun.
He stood still and waited. If ever
The hour of revelation was come
It was now, here on the transfigured steep.
The sky darkened. Some birds chirped. Nothing else.
He thought the dying god had gone to sleep :
An Indian fakir on his mat of nails.

V

And on the summit of the asphalt road
Which stretched towards the fiery town, the man
Saw one hill raised like a hairy arm, dark
With pines and cedars against the stricken sun
– The arm of Moses or of Joshua.
He dropped his head and let fall the halo
Of mountains, purpling and silent as time,
To see temptation coiled before his feet :
A violated grass snake that lugged
Its intestine like a small red valise.

A cold-eyed skinflint it now was, and not
The manifest of that joyful wisdom,
The mirth and arrogant green flame of life;
Or earth's vivid tongue that flicked in praise of earth.

VI

And the man wept because pity was useless.
"Your jig's up; the flies come like kites," he said
And watched the grass snake crawl towards the hedge,
Convulsing and dragging into the dark
The satchel filled with curses for the earth,
For the odours of warm sedge, and the sun,
A blood-red organ in the dying sky.
Backwards it fell into a grassy ditch
Exposing its underside, white as milk,
And mocked by wisps of hay between its jaws;
And then it stiffened to its final length.
But though it opened its thin mouth to scream
A last silent scream that shook the black sky,
Adamant and fierce, the tall man did not curse.

VII

Beside the rigid snake the man stretched out
In fellowship of death; he lay silent
And stiff in the heavy grass with eyes shut,
Inhaling the moist odours of the night
Through which his mind tunnelled with flicking tongue
Backwards to caves, mounds, and sunken ledges
And desolate cliffs where come only kites,
And where of perished badgers and racoons
The claws alone remain, gripping the earth.
Meanwhile the green snake crept upon the sky,
Huge, his mailed coat glittering with stars that made
The night bright, and blowing thin wreaths of cloud
Athwart the moon; and as the weary man
Stood up, coiled above his head, transforming all.

The Well-Wrought Urn

"What would you do
    if I suddenly died?"

"Write a poem to you."

"Would you mourn for me?"

"Certainly," I sighed.

"For a long time?"

"That depends."

"On what?"

"The poem's excellence," I replied.

MARGARET
AVISON

Margaret Avison spent some of her early years in Alberta, but
was born in 1918 at Galt, Ontario, attended Victoria College
at the University of Toronto, and since her graduation in 1940
(BA' in English Language and Literature) has lived in Toronto
more often than not, employed variously as secretary,
research assistant, librarian, etc. She was a Guggenheim
Fellow in Poetry for 1956–57.

During the forties Miss Avison's poetry appeared occasionally
in Canadian magazines (*Canadian Forum, Contemporary
Verse, Here and Now*) and during the fifties more commonly
in American ones (*Poetry*, Chicago, *Origin, Kenyon Review*),
but her only collection is *Winter Sun* (University of Toronto
Press, 1960). A list of poems printed in magazines and
anthologies before the end of 1959 can be found in *Canadian
Literature* (Autumn, 1959), to which can now be added the
groups in *Poetry 62* (The Ryerson Press, 1961) and in *Origin*

(January, 1962). She has been characterized by her critics in
very different ways: as imagist and intellectual, as space-
traveller and city-poet, as aloof scholar and compassionate
humanitarian, among other things. Her total published
output to date is less than a hundred poems, but since the
early forties she has continuously maintained her reputation
as one of the handful of current writers that no reader of
Canadian poetry ought to neglect.

❖

The Valiant Vacationist

When we started to climb those steps,
Stone steps up and echoing round and up,
I felt genteel enough, mistaking it for Brock's monument.

    I don't remember why I knew
    That woman we met (she was coming down)
    Would never never never find the bottom.

Anyway, I knew at once
That this dutiful interlude would not be followed
By squashed-egg sandwiches and coca-cola.
Up till then we had never suspected
That there were any alternatives
To a picnic lunch in the park,
Beside the car, well away from the public toilets.

    But here, on a half-way landing
    An old fly guzzled a dirty windowpane:
    I wanted to shake his hand or clap him on the shoulder
    As my last countryman, and I could have cried
    Because our hands were so far not the same
    In size and shape and custom. And I knew
    He didn't notice, and didn't even care.

After that landing came the wooden steps
With broken edges, and here and there
A crushed lily, a piece of old seaweed,
Smashed chalk of shells ground up with sawdust
And the naked air showing through –

    And then, to the right, a river-bank
    Thin with young birches, where an old white horse
Grazed absently. The path led to the bridge
Slung over the sliding river's cloudy green
(Like an evening over your shoulder in early May)

Then the wooden steps again, and far below
The scrag and cliff. And then a morning pool
Misty, verging into the quicksand flats.

    The word I send from here
    Is pitched so fine it lances my tympanum
    And I begin to wonder whether you hear it?

    Moreover, last night's stars were plash
    On my enamelled skull, and now I smell
    The morgue-dawn will be snow, but myriad.

In the meantime anyway it might be wise
If I made arrangements only for myself
When I arrive. Then, if you come, we can surely
Find accommodation without any trouble.
I haven't met any tourists since last Sunday
    Nor anyone else in fact.
Perhaps you'd better wait till you hear again.
Frost burns so quickly and the sun today
Was yellower than you are used to see it.
    Their language here you wouldn't understand.
    Myself, I find it difficult
        and so far have been unsuccessful
           in finding anyone
                Even to interpret for me to myself.
When I have mastered it, I'll let you know.

Perspective

A sport, an adventitious sprout
These eyeballs, that have somehow slipped
The mesh of generations since Mantegna?

Yet I declare, your seeing is diseased
That cripples space. The fear has eaten back
Through sockets to the caverns of the brain
    And made of it a sifty habitation.

We stand beholding the one plain
And in your face I see the chastening
Of its small tapering design
That brings up *punkt*.
    (The Infinite, you say,
    Is an unthinkable – and pointless too –
        Extension of that *punkt*.)

But ho you miss the impact of that fierce
Raw boulder five miles off? You are not pierced
By that great spear of grass on the horizon?
    You are not smitten with the shock
        Of that great thundering sky?

Your law of optics is a quarrel
Of chickenfeet on paper. Does a train
Run pigeon-toed?

I took a train from here to Ottawa
On tracks that did not meet. We swelled and roared
Mile upon mightier mile, and when we clanged
Into the vasty station we were indeed
Brave company for giants.

    Keep your eyes though,
You, and not I, will travel safer back
                To Union station.

Your fear has me infected, and my eyes
That were my sport so long, will soon be apt
Like yours to press out dwindling vistas from
The massive flux massive Mantegna knew
And all its sturdy everlasting foregrounds.

❖

The Iconoclasts

The dervish dancer on the smoking steppes
Unscrolled, into the level lava-cool
Of Romish twilight, baleful hyroglyphs
That had been civic architecture,
    The sculptured utterances of the Schools.

The Vikings rode the tasseled sea :
Over their shoulders, running towards their boats,
They had seen the lurking matriarchal wolves,
Ducked their bright foreheads from the iron laurels
Of a dark Scandinavian destiny,
And chosen, rather, to be dwarfed to pawns
    Of the broad sulking sea.

And Lampman, when he prowled the Gatineau :
Were the white vinegar of northern rivers,
The stain of punkwood in chill evening air,
The luminous nowhere past the gloomy hills,
Were these his April cave –
    Sought as the first men, when the bright release
    Of sun filled them with sudden self-disdain
    At bone-heaps, rotting pelts, muraled adventures,
    Sought a more primitive nakedness?

The cave-men, Lampman, Lief, the dancing dervish,
Envied the fleering wolf his secret circuit;
   But knew their doom to propagate, create,
   Their wild salvation wrapt within that white
   Burst of pure art whose only premise was
   Ferocity in them, thudding its dense
   Distracting rhythms down their haunted years.

❖

From a Provincial

Bent postcards come from Interlaken
In August, the tired emperor of the year;
On evening tables
Midges survey their planes of brief discovery
At a half-run. In Milton's candle's light
They so employed themselves.
Some die before the light is out.
Between darkness and darkness
Every small valley shows a familiar compass
Until like all before
Still most unknown, it vanishes.
In Caesar's camp was order,
The locus of their lives for some centurions
Encircled by forests of sombre France.
When day and life draw the horizons
Part of the strangeness is
Knowing the landscape.

New Year's Poem

The Christmas twigs crispen and needles rattle
Along the windowledge.
      A solitary pearl
Shed from the necklace spilled at last week's party
Lies in the suety, snow-luminous plainness
Of morning, on the windowledge beside them.
And all the furniture that circled stately
And hospitable when these rooms were brimmed
With perfumes, furs, and black-and-silver
Crisscross of seasonal conversation, lapses
Into its previous largeness.
      I remember
Anne's rose-sweet gravity, and the stiff grave
Where cold so little can contain;
I mark the queer delightful skull and crossbones
Starlings and sparrows left, taking the crust,
And the long loop of winter wind
Smoothing its arc from dark Arcturus down
To the bricked corner of the drifted courtyard,
And the still windowledge.
      Gentle and just pleasure
It is, being human, to have won from space
This unchill, habitable interior
Which mirrors quietly the light
Of the snow, and the new year.

That Eureka of Archimedes out of his bath
Is the kind of story that kills what it conveys;
Yet the banality is right for that story, since it is not a
    communicable one
But just a particular instance of
The kind of lighting up of the terrain
That leaves aside the whole terrain, really,
But signalizes, and compels, an advance in it
Such an advance through a be-it-what-it-may but take-it-not-
    quite-as-given locale :
Probably that is the core of being alive.
The speculation is not a concession
To limited imaginations. Neither is it
A constrained voiding of the quality of immanent death.
Such near values cannot be measured in values
Just because the measuring
Consists in that other kind of lighting up
That shows the terrain comprehended, as also its containing
    space,
And wipes out adjectives, and all shadows
                        (or, perhaps, all but shadows).

The Russians made a movie of a dog's head
Kept alive by blood controlled by physics, chemistry,
    equipment, and
Russian women scientists in cotton gowns with writing
    tablets.
The heart lay on a slab midway in the apparatus
And went phluff, phluff.
Like the first kind of illumination, that successful experiment
Can not be assessed either as conquest or as defeat.
But it is living, creating the chasm of creation,
Contriving to cast only man to brood in it, further.

History makes the spontaneous jubilation at such moments
    less and less likely though,
And that story about Archimedes does get into public school
    textbooks.

From rooming-house to rooming-house
The toasted evening spells
City to hayrick, warming and bewildering
A million motes. From gilded tiers,
Balconies, and sombre rows,
Women see gopher-hawks, and rolling flaxen hills;
Smell a lost childhood's homely supper.
Men lean with folded newspapers,
Touched by a mushroom and root-cellar
Coolness. The wind flows,
Ruffles, unquickens. Crumbling ash
Leaves the west chill. The Sticks-&-Stones, this City,
Lies funeral bare.
Over its gaping arches stares
That haunt, the mirror mineral.
In cribs, or propped at plastic tablecloths,
Children are roundeyed, caught by a cold magic,
Fading of glory. In their dim
Cement-floored garden the zoo monkeys shiver.
Doors slam. Lights snap, restore
The night's right prose.
Gradually
All but the lovers' ghostly windows close.

Snow

Nobody stuffs the world in at your eyes.
The optic heart must venture : a jail-break
And re-creation. Sedges and wild rice
Chase rivery pewter. The astonished cinders quake
With rhizomes. All ways through the electric air
Trundle candy-bright disks; they are desolate
Toys if the soul's gates seal, and cannot bear,
Must shudder under, creation's unseen freight.
But soft, there is snow's legend : colour of mourning
Along the yellow Yangtze where the wheel
Spins an indifferent stasis that's death's warning.
Asters of tumbled quietness reveal
Their petals. Suffering this starry blur
The rest may ring your change, sad listener.

❖

Butterfly Bones; or Sonnet
Against Sonnets

The cyanide jar seals life, as sonnets move
towards final stiffness. Cased in a white glare
these specimens stare for peering boys, to prove
strange certainties. Plane dogsled and safari
assure continuing range. The sweep-net skill,
the patience, learning, leave all living stranger.
Insect – or poem – waits for the fix, the frill
precision can effect, brilliant with danger.
What law and wonder the museum spectres
bespeak is cryptic for the shivery wings,
the world cut-diamond-eyed, those eyes' reflectors,
or herbal grass, sunned motes, fierce listening.
Might sheened and rigid trophies strike men blind
like Adam's lexicon locked in the mind?

Meeting together of Poles and Latitudes (In Prospect)

Those who fling off, toss head,
    Taste the bitter morning, and have at it –
    Thresh, knead, dam, weld,
    Wave baton, force
    Marches through squirming bogs,
    Not from contempt, but
    From thrust, unslakeably thirsty,
    Amorous of every tower and twig, and
    Yet like railroad engines with
    Longings for their landscapes (pistons pounding)
    Rock fulminating through
    Wrecked love, unslakeably loving –
    Seldom encounter at the Judgment Seat
Those who are flung off, sit
    Dazed awhile, gather concentration,
    Follow vapour-trails with shrivelling wonder,
    Pilfer, mow, play jongleur
    With mathematic signs, or
    Tracing the forced marches make
    Peculiar cats-cradles of telephone wire,
    Lap absently at sundown, love
    As the stray dog on foreign hills
    A bone-myth, atavistically,
    Needing more faith, and fewer miles, but
    Slumber-troubled by it,
    Wanting for death that
    Myth-clay, though
    Scratch-happy in these (foreign) brambly wilds;
But when they approach each other
    The place is an astonishment :
    Runways shudder with little planes
    Practising folk-dance steps or
    Playing hornet,
    Sky makes its ample ruling
    Clear as a primary child's exercise-book
    In somebody else's language,

And the rivers under the earth
Foam without whiteness, domed down,
As they foam indifferently every
Day and night (if you'd call that day and night)
Not knowing how they wait, at the node, the
Curious encounter.

❖

Mordent for a Melody

Horsepower crops Araby for pasture.
TV glides past the comet's fin.
No question, time is moving faster
And, maybe, space is curling in.

Seething with atoms, trifles show
The Milky Way in replica.
Clip but a fingernail, and lo!
A supernova drops away.

Spinning ourselves at stunning speed,
Within our envelope of air
We spin again. The derricks bleed
To spark us round and round our sphere.

Things are arranged in series. What
Appears but once we never see.
Yet someone, streaking by then, caught
Crescendoes of conformity.

Reported them a unit, proved
Proliferation serves its turn.
(How can the Engineer above
Refuel, at the rate we burn?)

Sleep has a secret tempo. Man
Swerves back to it, out of the glare,
And finds that each recurring dawn
Wakes Rip Van Winkles everywhere.

Dance of the midges in the warm
Sand reaches of infinity,
May this invisible music swarm
Our spirits, make them hep, and we

Sing with our busy wings a gay
Pas de million until our singeing-day.

❖

On the Death of France Darte Scott

UPON THE BIRTH OF TWIN SONS WHO LATER DIED

For the gemini, lost in the womb
Of the fair May mother lost in the snow
In the wintry wastes the ancient alone should know
There is vastly room
From the mortal dominions yielded;
But not where the fields are gilded
With buttercups and the children's sun.
The purple arc of the polar night
Inscribes horizon for them, where light
Would nightless glow, could the winter wane
Before that winter inspire the twain
With the frore May mother's mortal chill.
The seven-months' boys are borne to ride
A snow-melled limitless flood of morning's tide
Who should, by a greening hill,
Sleep warm and still.

The others, not strange yet, not forlorn,
Sundered in summer, only themselves can mourn.

Birth Day

Saturday I ran to Mitilene.

Bushes and glass along the grass-still way
Were all dabbled with rain
And the road reeled with shattered skies.

Towards noon an inky, petulant wind
Ravelled the pools, and rinsed the black grass round them.

Gulls were up in the late afternoon
And the air gleamed and billowed
And broadcast flung astringent spray
                              All swordy-silver.
I saw the hills lie brown and vast and passive.

The men of Mitilene waited restive
Until the yellow melt of sun.
I shouted out my news as I sped towards them
That all, rejoicing, could go down to dark.

All nests, with all moist downy young
Blinking and gulping daylight; and all lambs
Four-braced in straw, shivering and mild;
And the first blood-root up from the ravaged beaches
Of the old equinox; and frangible robins' blue
Teethed right around to sun :
These first we loudly hymned;
And then
The hour of genesis
When first the moody firmament
Swam out of Arctic chaos,
Orbed solidly as the huge frame for this
Cramped little swaddled creature's coming forth
To slowly, foolishly, marvellously
Discover a unique estate, held wrapt
Away from all men else, which to embrace
Our world would have to stretch and swell with strangeness.

This made us smile, and laugh at last. There was
Rejoicing all night long in Mitilene.

Dispersed Titles

[FLIGHT]

Through the bleak hieroglyphs
of chart and table
thumb-tacked for winnowed navigators
who stroke the sable air,
earth's static-electric fur,
who ride it, bucked or level,
master it with minerals gouged and fabricated
out of it, insist
on being part of it, gouged out,
denatured nature, subject
to laws self-corrugated,
created out of it,
through these hieroglyphs and chart
mark with the hearing of the eye
the bellrung hours of Tycho Brahe.

[HAS ROOTS]

He – Kepler's Orpheus –
a Danish crown, the bishops,
the snarling North Sea night,
bakers of biscuit,
ladies, sweet ladies,
stuffed in their cabinets, swollen with toothache,
the straw and bran
unfabling fields already,
while the Narcissus sun
lends clods a shining :
All somewhere, still,
though they seem lost away
from their wierd hollow under the solar architrave.

BUT IS CUT OFF

Are they all only in
those other hieroglyphs
of the created, solitary brain?
borne here in a man-toy?
bounced up, a ball
that chooses when to fall,
comets for hap,
a new respect for the extremes?

Something wrought by itself out of itself
must bear its own
ultimates of heat and cold
nakedly, refusing
the sweet surrender.
Old Mutabilitie has been
encompassed too, wrought into
measures of climbing and elipse.
This little fierce fabrique
seals the defiant break
with cycles, for old Tycho Brahe's sake.

EXCEPT FROM ALL ITS SELVES

But soft! (o curly Tudor) –
No pith of history will
be cratered in one skull.

The continents, my brother Buckminster
no cramp of will comprises.
The oak that cracked a quilted tumulus
and rustled, all through childhood's
lacey candle-drip of winter,
through feathered morning hours, later
through glass, so that the glassy
exultation of an articulate

stripped rock-and-ribs,
an intellect
created into world, was
wounded with whispers from a single oak-tree.

> The periwinkle eyes
> of seaborde men
> too young for gladness
> fade with their shanties.
> Lost, like the committing of sins,
> crag-shapes are sediment,
> chopped down, minced, poured to pave
>   the shelving
> parade ground for pinioned grotesques
> in the pink shadow-lengthening
> barracks of evening.

THE EARTH HAS OTHER ROOTS AND SELVES

For Tycho Brahe's sake I find myself,
but lose myself again for
so few are salvaged
in the sludge of the
ancestral singular.

> Ancestral? Even my brother
> walks under waving plumes of strangeness.
> The northern centuries
> funnel me, a chute of
> steel and water tumbling,
> and I forget
> warm boards, old market awnings,
> the two fat little feet in shawls
> treading a beaded woman's easy arm
> by a sunned stone,
> a ginger root
> in a stone jar,
> a lattice-work of iron
> in a dry wind, overlooking

fuchsia flats and the
scorched Moorish mountains,
or holy peaks frilled with cirrus ice
and the slick-paper blues and greens
of their flanks rich
with floral forest.

THE NAMELESS ONE DWELLS IN HIS TENTS

Forget much more . . .
a name, not the made-name
corrupted to man-magic, to fend off
the ice, the final fire of this
defiance.

Things I can't know I smell
as plainly as if invisible campfires
smoked : a hum of sightless suppers
on the irridescent shore
under the dunes. The wanderer's
sandals ship, and shift, cool sand.

AND "UP" IS A DIRECTION

Because one paces (none, now, strut)
one faces sea and space and is
tempted to think : Proscenium !
We have revolted.

Only the stagestruck mutter still
to the night's empty galleries.
Tossed out in the confused up-and-down
too many have casually
fingered the gilt loge fringes,
snuffed into dust the
dessicated peanut-shells
since the last true audition,
and found not even ghosts even in the echoing foyer.

To Professor X, Year Y

The square for civic receptions
Is jammed, static, black with people in topcoats
Although November
Is mean, and day grows late.

The newspapermen, who couldn't
Force their way home, after the council meeting
&c., move between windows and pressroom
In ugly humour. They do not know
What everybody is waiting for
At this hour
To stand massed and unmoving
When there should be – well – nothing to expect
Except the usual hubbub
Of city five o'clock.

Winter pigeons walk the cement ledges
Urbane, discriminating.

Down in the silent crowd few can see anything.
It is disgusting, this uniformity
Of stature.
If only someone climbed in pyramid
As circus families can . . .
Strictly, each knows
Downtown buildings block all view anyway
Except, to tease them,
Four narrow passages, and ah
One clear towards open water
(If "clear"
 Suits with the prune and mottled plumes of
 Madam night).

Nobody gapes skyward
Although the notion of
Commerce by air is utterly
familiar.

Many citizens at this hour
Are of course miles away, under
Rumpus-room lamps, dining-room chandeliers,
Or bound elsewhere.
One girl who waits in a lit drugstore doorway
North 48 blocks for the next bus
Carries a history, an ethics, a Russian grammar,
And a pair of gym shoes.

But the few thousand inexplicably here
Generate funny currents, zigzag
Across the leaden miles, and all suburbia
Suffers, uneasily.

You, historian, looking back at us,
Do you think I'm not trying to be helpful?
If I fabricated cause-and-effect
You'd listen? I've been dead too long for fancies.
Ignore us, hunched in these dark streets
If in a minute now the explosive
Meaning fails to disperse us and provide resonance
Appropriate to your chronicle.

But if you do, I have a hunch
You've missed a portent.
("Twenty of six." "Snow? – I wouldn't wonder.")

Intra-Political

Who are we here?
boxed, bottled, barrelled
in rows?
Comestibles with the trick
of turning grocer, shoplifter
or warehouse trucker, or sometimes,
in faery-false springtime
the lion-hearted four-foot haggler
with a hot dime?

Games are too earnest.
These packaged us-es
are to the gamboling of real nourishment
as mudcake to transmuted sun.
Truth is, men chew and churn (in rows
or squares, or one by one
like a domino on a walled tennis-court)
galactic courses:
chlorophyll, mutton, mineral salts
pinpoint multiple sunrise, and
cram us with incendiary force;
or we ingesting cede
the solar plexus its serenes of sky,
till every sunborn creature
may lume deepforest pools, and floodlight
his architects; find, too,
lenses for micro-astronomical
amaze (he – transport! –
SNEEZES).

Who plunges away
from the inexorable of
weaving orbits, like a colt
hurtled from his gentle pasturing
by a through freight?
(Space with its purple eye
marks his fixed field
and not his helter-skelter heels.)

Fixity of our sun-selves in our courses –
that willed harmonics – is
nothing we know to date,
nothing we know
who do know fearful things.

Look at that platinum moon,
the sky still muslin pale inspiring
doom-sweet violation.
But ask the lone balloonist.
Zones of ultramarine
clutch at his jugular,
and when he engineers his venture,
a Vandal, loving, he lays waste;
the fields and folds Horace could celebrate
strip back to rainsoak
and Rome still baldly suns in its
imperial distances.
(Nothing inert may, in stone, space, exist – except as
 our clocking selves insert it.
 We move too far from ways of weightlessness.)
Space is a hazard.

Yet this pre-creation density
presses : our darkness dreams of
this heavy mass, this moil, this self-
consuming endless squirm and squander, this
chaos, singling off
in a new Genesis.
(Would it perhaps set swinging
 the little horn-gates to new life's
 illumined labyrinths if, released
 from stifling,
 creatures like us were planet-bathed
 in new-born Light?)
(Glee dogs our glumness so.)

Dreams, even doubted, drive us.
Our games and grocery-store designs
are nursery-earnest,

evidence.
Strait thinking set us down in rows
and rigged the till.
But being bought and eaten
is, experienced, enough
to change this circular exchange.
And cringeing from such courses
compounds confusion :
a new numerical excess
of us-es.

We set up shop after,
poach as we might, nothing else much remained
but tufts of fur and insect skeletons?
And energy hasn't minded
phoenixing for us in our nonce?

But even our own energy
will out. String beans
and coronal pyres of sleep
keg up. These city shelves,
this play emporium,
wobble on nitroglycerine.

If, with dainty stepping, we unbox ourselves
while still Explosion slumbers,
putting aside mudcakes,
the buying, selling, trucking, packaging
of mudcakes,
sun-stormed, daring to gambol,
might there not be an immense answering
of human skies?
a new expectant largeness?
Form has its flow,
a Heraclitus-river with no riverbank
we can play poise on now.

(George Herbert – and he makes it plain –
 Guest at this same transfiguring board
        Did sit and eat.)

Thaw

Sticky inside their winter suits
The Sunday children stare at pools
In pavement and black ice where roots
Of sky in moodier sky dissolve.

An empty coach train runs along
The thin and sooty river flats
And stick and straw and random stones
Steam faintly when its steam departs.

Lime-water and licorice light
Wander the tumbled streets. A few
Sparrows gather. A dog barks out
Under the dogless pale pale blue.

Move your tongue along a slat
Of a raspberry box from last year's crate.
Smell a saucepantilt of water
On the coal-ash in your grate.

Think how the Black Death made men dance,
And from the silt of centuries
The proof is now scraped bare that once
Troy fell and Pompey scorched and froze.

A boy alone out in the court
Whacks with his hockey-stick, and whacks
In the wet, and the pigeons flutter, and rise,
And settle back.

The Local & the Lakefront

The crankle can occur
in stunted trees:
a shaping line, when rain blackens the
bark, in early
spring, in Scarborough
(Toronto, East).

At Sunnyside
Toronto lakefront, west,
      with a bricked sooted railwaystation and
              a blueglass busstation)
the sunset
blurges through rain and all
man tinfoil, man sheetlead
shines, angled all awry,
a hoaxing hallelujah.

Wharves
spidered in mist
I, stevedore of the spirit,
slog day and night, picketing
those barges and brazen freighters with their
Subud, Sumerian ramsgate, entrails and altars.

Grievance – grievance –
Committeeman, come where I pace
and learn my rain-besotted, rancorous
grievance.
Who that must die but man
can burn a bush to make a bar of soap?
Who twists a draughtsman's line
perversely, out of
a stunted tree,
or makes of the late sun an as-if-Gabriel
to trump
another day, another borough?
Someone not at home. Exporters. Glutting us
with Danish spoons
and aum.

On the flossed beaches here
we're still curling our waves.
Weather is tough.
Things happen only to trees and the
rivering grasses.
A person is an alien.

Committeeman :
there are no ships or cargoes *there*.
Believe me. Look. Admit it.
Then we start clean :
   nothing earned; a nowhere to exchange
        among us few
           carefully.

❖

Waking Up

Monkey colour, morning smokes from
the pond. Looped and festooned
with fawn heraldic rags
trees wait. Seawall of day
deafens the turmoil the true seafarer,
the Wanderer, fronts. High grass
rides crest; a spill
of grains casts stone-age shadows on the bluffs.
Selvedge of water mirrors
the always first light.
Like soil no inchworm's excremental course
has rendered friable,
today, mute quantum
of all past pitted against sun,
weighs, a heft of awareness, on
tallow, brawn, auricle,

iris. Till monkey-
grinder habit turning his organ
grinds out curbs, scurrying,
dust,
day.

❖

Holiday Plans for the
Whole Family

When daylight is broad
quarter the candytuft
into the wheelbarrow.
From the east border.

   Mariners may be looked for on monorails
   with heads like Paynims.

Those miniature pasteboard buckets are poor
coffee containers; the toothpicks in that store though
are peppermint flavoured; wrapped; one per parcel.

   Gardening need not be hobbied.
   To be anhungered and of good appetite
   calls for long learning.

A star-map and a stone jar
of cool pebbles to roll in cellared sound
will have to do with daylight.

Simon (finis)

Not the leaf-crisp wind but the
cotton-thin
in a wheat-silvered sky.
Spruce cones are sieves to the clear
cold, as are cliffs,
shingles, men
in the meadowing day.

Bone rick man on an iron cot
under the singling shingles, high
by sky-light hears a cement-mixer
tumble and grind
and is wise.

Salmon-cold hands on the hod and the steady
shoring of hours
humped through a life-time
touches him, laid out now in his tatters
to a gradual smile.

RAYMOND

SOUSTER

Raymond Souster was born in Toronto in 1921 and attended public school and high school there. After serving in the RCAF from 1941 to 1945 he returned to Toronto, where he now works as a banker. In addition to writing poems of his own, Souster has always been a very active member of the poetic community. He edited and circulated a mimeographed periodical called *Combustion* for a number of years, combined with Louis Dudek and Irving Layton to produce a collection of their verse called *Cerberus* (1952) and is a leading editor of Contact Press, the poets' co-operative which has been responsible for printing a remarkable number of important books by Canadian poets during the past ten years. But Souster's poetic community is as much North American as Canadian, and his acquaintance with United States poets and poetry is both wide and close.

Souster was one of the young poets represented in *Unit of Five* (The Ryerson Press, 1944) and since then he has produced over ten books of his own, including *The Selected Poems* (Contact Press, 1956), chosen by Louis Dudek from the work of the previous twelve years, *Place of Meeting* (Gallery Editions, 1962) and *A Local Pride* (Contact Press, 1962). The Ryerson Press expects to publish Souster's *Collected Poems* in 1964. Although he has been associated with some of Canada's most factional writers, Souster's own work is more notable for unifying than splitting the public. It finds its steadily growing band of supporters among readers of remarkably various tastes, opinions, and backgrounds.

❖

The Hunter

I carry the groundhog along by the tail
All the way back to the farm, with the blood
Dripping out of his mouth a couple of drops at a time,
Leaving a perfect trail for anyone to follow.

The half-wit hired-man is blasting imaginary rabbits
Somewhere on our left; we walk through fields steaming after rain
Jumping the mud; I watch the swing of your girl's hip in the cotton dress
Ahead of me, the proud way your hand holds the gun, and remembering how you held it
Up to the hog caught in the trap, and blew his head in,

Wonder what fate you have in store for me.

Night Watch

Not at Angelo's with wine and spaghetti,
Not at the Oak Room, not at Joe's, Mabel's, or Tim's Place,
Enclosed by no four walls, circled by no chatter, held by
    no unseen hands of music;

But here with the lean cold pushing the dim light from the
    stars,
Here under ghost buildings, here with silence grown too
    silent;

You and I in the doorway like part of a tomb,
Kissing the night with bitter cigarettes.

❖

Poem for her Picture

Behind you the lake, the boat, the sand,
But I cannot see past your body dressed in its covering,
Cannot see past your upturned hair, your smile.

You need no backgrounds,
No one would see them anyway.

O my warm goddess,
Step down from the wall
And we will span the blackness of two years
In our eyes' and our lips' first touching together.

Search

Not another bite, not another cigarette,
Nor a final coffee from the shining coffee-urn before you
    leave
The warmth steaming at the windows of the hamburger-
    joint where the Wurlitzer
Booms all night without a stop, where the onions are thick
    between the buns.
Wrap yourself well in that cheap coat that holds back the
    wind like a sieve,
You have a long way to go, and the streets are dark, you
    may have to walk all night before you find
Another heart as lonely, so nearly mad with boredom, so
    filled with such strength, such tenderness of love.

❖

Nice People

Nice people, these intellectuals – when they become tired
With life as it must be lived they invent fantasies, or
                  worse – this

Gathering in a high loft of a room, everybody drunk
Or on the way to it with glassfuls of Scotch, and in the
                  centre

A huge old-fashioned brass bed on which
The chorus-girls invited for the evening take turns
With the gentlemen still capable of intercourse. While
                  the poet

Sits gravely in the back kitchen, arguing with the negro maid
(Almost an intellectual herself) the pros and cons
Of sterilizing the family cat now curled in the centre of
                  the floor.

Lagoons: Hanlan's Point

Mornings
Before the sun's liquid
Spilled gradually, flooding
The island's cool cellar,
There was the boat
And the still lagoons,
With the sound of my oars
The only intrusion
Over cries of birds
In the marshy shallows
Or the loud thrashing
Of the startled crane
Rushing the air.

And in one strange
Dark, tree-hung entrance,
I followed the sound
Of my heart all the way
To its reed-blocked ending,
With the pads of the lily
Thick as greenshining film
Covering the water.

And in another
Where the sun came
To probe the depths
Through a shaft of branches,
I saw the skeletons
Of brown ships rotting
Far below in their burial-ground,
And wondered what strange fish
With what stranger colours
Swam through these places
Under the water . . .

A small boy
With a flat-bottomed punt
And an old pair of oars
Moving in wonder
Through the antechamber
Of a waking world.

❖

The Bourgeois Child

I might have been a slum child,
I might have learned to swear and steal,
I might have learned to drink and whore.

But I was raised a good bourgeois child
And so it has taken me a little longer.

❖

Study: The Bath

In the almost subdued light
Of the bathroom a woman
Steps from white tub
Towel around her shoulders.

Drops of water glisten
On her body, slight buttocks,
Neck, the tight belly,
Fall at intervals
From the slightly plumed
Oval of crotch.

Neck bent forward
Eyes collected
All her attention gathered
At the ends of fingers

As she removes the superfluous
Dead skin from her nipples.

✤

The Attack

Only last night Pat was attacked
By three young punks. He was going
By the cemetery when they jumped him,
Dragged him inside behind some tombstones
And beat him up good. "For a while," he told me,
"I thought they might even kill me, and I remember thinking
What a hell of a place to be found dead in."

✤

Girl at the Corner of Elizabeth and Dundas

You want it or you don't
You got five bucks or no
I'm twenty-one I ain't
Got any time to waste
You want it or you don't
Make up your jesus mind.

Downtown Corner News-Stand

It will need all of death to take you from this corner.
It has become your world, and you its unshaved
Bleary-eyed, foot-stamping king. In winter
You curse the cold, huddled in your coat from the wind,
You fry in summer like an egg hopping on a griddle,
And always the whining voice, the nervous-flinging arms,
The red face, the shifting eyes watching, waiting
Under the grimy cap for God knows what
To happen. (But nothing ever does; downtown
Toronto goes to sleep and wakes the next morning
Always the same, except a little dirtier.)
And you stand with your armful of Stars and Telys,
The peak of your cap well down against the sun,
And all the city's restless, seething river
Surges beside you, but not once do you plunge
Into its flood, or are carried or tossed away :
But reappear always, beard longer than ever, nose running,
To catch the noon editions at King and Bay.

❖

Flight of the Roller-Coaster

Once more around should do it, the man confided . . .

And sure enough, when the roller-coaster reached the peak
Of the giant curve above me, screech of its wheels
Almost drowned by the shriller cries of the riders –

Instead of the dip and plunge with its landslide of screams
It rose in the air like a movieland magic carpet, some
    wonderful bird,

And without fuss or fanfare swooped slowly across the
    amusement park,
Over Spook's Castle, ice-cream booths, shooting-gallery;
    and losing no height

Made the last yards above the beach, where the cucumber-
    cool
Brakeman in the last seat saluted
A lady about to change from her bathing-suit.

Then, as many witnesses duly reported, headed leisurely
    over the water,
Disappearing mysteriously all too soon behind a low-lying
    flight of clouds.

❖

The Need for Roots

If all of us
Who need roots
Start digging
At the same time

There just aren't
Going to be enough spades
To go around.

Night After Rain

After the day-long rain
Each tree seems to have a bird in it singing
Its fool head off
                    and why not, the little buggers
Have their bellies choked up with worms, are almost dizzy
With the sight of so many floating in every gutter.

And looking up to see the birds
I notice shy traces of buds,
The little green fronds on the willows

And feel as I go up the street
Almost ashamed of my sorrow.

❖

My Brother Dying

As he looks down at us
With his fear-glazed eyes,
Does he picture us buzzards
Circling round his bed,
Waiting patiently
For his death and his bones?

No: just his mother, his brother,
Who could do nothing for him
When he sat with the living,
And can do nothing now
As he crawls toward death.

The Thing

You've come here to die.
I read it in your eyes
Which look through and past me
To The Thing by the bed,

Which keeps nodding its head
In its Yes Yes Yes.

❖

At the House of Hambourg

Hardly had we groped our way
Through the fog of this cellar of boredom,
When huge drops of loneliness began to drip from the
    ceiling,
(This was caught, we learned later, by the management,
And served to the customers as near beer),
And even Moe Kaufman couldn't drive the curse away
As he rode out hot through the coitus of the reed
With candle flames licking like mad
The most secret parts of the walls.

❖

The Six Quart Basket

The six quart basket
One side gone
Half the handle torn off

Sits in the centre of the lawn
And slowly fills up
With the white fruits of the snow.

❖

The Top Hat

Whether it's just a gag or the old geezer's
A bit queer in the head, it's still refreshing
To see someone walking up Bay Street
With toes out of shoes, patched trousers, frayed suit-coat,
And on his head the biggest shiniest top hat
Since Abe Lincoln
                        and walking as if the whole
Damn street belonged to him
                              which at this moment for my money
It does.

❖

Night on the Uplands

A fire on such a warm night?
Crazy, wasn't it, but then

The mosquitoes wanted our flesh
As much as we wanted each other!

And as I remember
Won out in the end.

At Split Rock Falls

At Split Rock Falls I first saw my death
In a sudden slip the space of a breath;
My windmill body met the crazy shock
Of uncounted centuries of stubborn rock.

At Split Rock Falls I saw green so green
It was as though grass had never been;
In the dappled depths of that pure pool
My face looked at me, recognized a fool.

From Split Rock Falls as I came away
The hint of a rainbow topped the spray,
And the trees tossed down : O let nothing matter
If not beautiful, swift as that singing water.

❖

The Coming of the Magi

In the tableau *The Coming of the Magi*
The Wise Men are seen at the entrance to the manger
Holding out precious gifts, gold,
Frankincense and myrrh, a look
Of awe and joy on their faces. . . .

                                      "Trouble with them guys",
He tells her, watching her last
Tantalizing twist from the girdle –
'They never had anything like this
To keep them home nights."

                                     "Like what?" she teases,

But he's looking out the window across to the church
Where the floodlights show up the awkward scene at the
manger.

"Like what?" she repeats, taking care rolling down the
second stocking.

"Like what, like what," he mocks her :
"Hell, think of them guys giving all that stuff
   To a kid like Jesus. . . ."

❖

The First Thin Ice

Tonight
our love-making

ducks
walking warily
the first thin ice
of winter.

❖

The Small White Cat

The small white cat
accepts the scraps of cheese
from my wife's fingers

then arching one paw
washes his face at once
as if to reward us.

Washroom Attendant

Your face flung at me
in the washroom mirror
sitting there slumped
in the shoeshine chair

is that of a dead man
who hasn't got the sense
to lie down and die,
rest with dignity :

instead must sit here
with a loud-mouthed band
hammering his ears
the eau de cologne
of piss in his nostrils

and if someone's drunk enough
a lousy quarter
for the best shine in town.

❖

The Proposition

The man coming toward us
is drunk : he stops us,
he's out of cigarettes,
and since he knows
you have to pay for everything
that nothing is ever free
and he hasn't a dime in his pockets,
he makes us a sporting proposition,
he offers us the use of his body
for our amusement
for our pleasure

and curses us, rightly,
when we laugh at him
and go on down the street

leaving him without cigarettes
without pride
without honour
without anything at all.

❖

Someone Has to Eat

Someone has to eat
the two-day old bread
the cans of peas
no one else wants

so here on Queen East
heavy with flies
coated with dust
ground under with heat

this tired food waits
its children of the shadows.

❖

Morning Certainly

Coming back from away out, a darkness,
there is light at the window,
my clothes are on the chair, as if waiting,
there is even
someone in bed with me.

Caterpillar

Caterpillar inching
up the sunward wall

I wish you tonight
same untroubled sleep

as my beloved
wrapped in dream's cocoon

then morning's first
thin stroke of dawn

laid on you soft
as this kiss I give
her sleepy lips now

caterpillar
of endearing patience
on the sunward wall.

❖

Invocation to the Muse

Goddess, I've watched too many
Of your loyal subjects go almost mad
With jealousy, disappointments, frustrations,
Not to wonder at all this waste
Of human effort and nerve-ends.

Nevertheless, desiring nothing
And expecting little, living only
For your secret inner praise, I give thanks
That you, goddess, out of so many
Should have chosen me for your cursed
And singular blessing.

The Child's Umbrella

What's it like to be homeless
all alone in this world?

Perhaps the jagged
ripped-open mouth
of the child's umbrella
lying inside out
on the winter pavement

can give us the answer.

JAMES

REANEY

James Reaney was born in 1926 on a farm near Stratford, Ontario. After graduating from Stratford Collegiate Institute, he attended the University of Toronto and graduated in English Language and Literature in 1948. An MA followed in 1949 and a PH.D in 1958. (His thesis on the relation of Spenser to Yeats was supervised by Northrop Frye, whose interest in the mythical patterns of literature he shares. He explains their significance for the Canadian poet in the June, 1959, issue of *Poetry*, Chicago.) For most of the fifties Reaney taught at the University of Manitoba, but in 1960 he moved to Middlesex College in the University of Western Ontario.

Reaney's early reputation was as a writer of short stories, but from 1947 his poetry started to appear in such Canadian magazines as *Northern Review* and *Contemporary Verse*, and in 1949 he collected a comparatively small segment of his early work in *The Red Heart* (McClelland and Stewart

Limited). Reaney's poems continued to appear in Canadian magazines, but few readers could have anticipated that his next book would be anything like *A Suit of Nettles* (The Macmillan Company, 1958), a sequence of pastoral eclogues, one for each month in the year (as in Spenser's *Shepheardes Calender*), in which the speakers are geese on an Ontario farm. His most recent poems are "A Message to Winnipeg" in *Poetry 62* (The Ryerson Press, 1961) and *Twelve Letters to a Small Town* (The Ryerson Press, 1962), the latter of which, like *The Red Heart*, harks back to his Stratford youth. Both "Message" and *Letters* were composed to be performed on the CBC with incidental music by John Beckwith.

Writing poetry has never stopped Reaney from writing other things, not merely short stories and sketches, but also critical studies of Isabella Valancy Crawford and Jay Macpherson, and an essay on "The Canadian Poet's Predicament" (*University of Toronto Quarterly*, April 1957). The chief rival to the poet, however, is the dramatist. In the past few years two plays, an opera (music by Beckwith), and a one-man masque have received a number of performances, on stage, radio, and television. Some of his work for theatre is collected in *The Killdeer and Other Plays* (The Macmillan Company, 1962). Reaney discusses his experience as a librettist and as a performer of his masque in "An Evening with Babble and Doodle" (*Canadian Literature*, Spring, 1962). He edits *Alphabet*, "A Semiannual devoted to the Iconography of the Imagination."

To the Avon River Above
Stratford, Canada

What did the Indians call you?
For you do not flow
With English accents.
I hardly know
What I should call you
    Because before
I drank coffee or tea
    I drank you
    With my cupped hands
And you did not taste English to me
    And you do not sound
    Like Avon
    Or swans & bards
But rather like the sad wild fowl
    In prints drawn
    By Audubon
And like dear bad poets
    Who wrote
    Early in Canada
And never were of note.
You are the first river
    I crossed
And like the first whirlwind
    The first rainbow
    First snow, first
    Falling star I saw,
You, for other rivers are my law.
    These other rivers:
    The Red & the Thames
    Are never so sweet
To skate upon, swim in
    Or for baptism of sin.
    Silver and light
The sentence of your voice,
    With a soprano

Continuous cry you shall
   Always flow
   Through my heart.
The rain and the snow of my mind
Shall supply the spring of that river
   Forever.
Though not your name
Your coat of arms I know
   And motto :
A shield of reeds and cresses
   Sedges, crayfishes
The hermaphroditic leech
Minnows, muskrats and farmers' geese
And printed above this shield
One of my earliest wishes
"To flow like you."

❖

Town House & Country Mouse

Old maids are the houses in town
They sit on streets like cement canals
   They are named after aldermen
     And their wives
   Or battles and dukes.

At a sky scratched with wires and smoke
They point their mild and weak gothic bonnets.
The houses of Albert and Brunswick Streets
Wait for farmers' barns to wed them
   But the streets are too narrow
     And they never come.

Out here barn is wedded to house,
   House is married to barn,
    Gray board and pink brick.
     The cowyard lies between
Where in winter on brown thin ice
    Red capped children skate.
   There is wallpaper in the house
      And in the barn
They are sawing the horns off a bull.

Out here the sound of bells on a wet evening
   Floating out clear when the wind is right.
    The factory whistles at noon in summer.
     Going from here to there
    As a child, not to a place with a name
     But first to get there :
The red buggy wheels move so fast
    They stand still
Whirling against sheaves of blue chicory
   The secret place where wild bees nest
The million leaning pens of grass with their nibs of seed,
    The wild rose bush – all
      Suddenly gone.
On gravel now where corduroy logs from the past
    Look dumbly up
Buried in the congregations of gravel,
     Getting closer the highway
     Cars darting back and forth
     In another world altogether.
Past the stonemason's house with its cement lion
   Not something to be very much afraid of
    Since it has legs like a table,
   Past the ten huge willows, the four poplars.
    Far away in a field the slaughterhouse,
     Two gas stations with windy signs,
The half world of the city outskirts : orchards
   Gone wild and drowned farms.
    Suddenly the square : –
People turning and shining like lighted jewels,

Terrifying sights : one's first nun !
   The first person with a wooden leg,
A huge chimney writing the sky
    With dark smoke.
     A parrot.
A clock in the shape of a man with its face
    In his belly
     The swan
A Dixie cup of ice cream with a wooden spoon

And then – backwards, the gas stations,
  The outskirts, orchards, slaughterhouse
  Far back the chimneys still writing
    Four poplars, ten huge willows
    The lion with table legs.
The bump as we go over old corduroy log
The gamut of grass and blue flowers
    Until the wheels stop
    And we are not uptown
     We are here
Where barn is wedded to house . . .
    Into town, out of town.

❖

The Royal Visit

When the King and the Queen came to Stratford
    Everyone felt at once
  How heavy the Crown must be.
The Mayor shook hands with their Majesties
  And everyone presentable was presented
  And those who weren't have resented
    It, and will
    To their dying day.
Everyone had almost a religious experience

When the King and Queen came to visit us
    (I wonder what they felt!)
And hydrants flowed water in the gutters
      All day.
People put quarters on the railroad tracks
So as to get squashed by the Royal Train
And some people up the line at Shakespeare
    Stayed in Shakespeare, just in case –
      They did stop too,
    While thousands in Stratford
      Didn't even see them
Because the Engineer didn't slow down
      Enough in time.
      And although,
But although we didn't see them in any way
    (I didn't even catch the glimpse
    The teacher who was taller did
      Of a gracious pink figure)
    I'll remember it to my dying
      Day.

❖

The Katzenjammer Kids

With porcupine locks
And faces which, when
More closely examined,
Are composed of measle-pink specks,
These two dwarf imps,
The Katzenjammer Kids,
Flitter through their Desert Island world.
Sometimes they get so out of hand
That a blue Captain
With stiff whiskers of black wicker
And an orange Inspector
With a black telescope

Pursue them to spank them
All through that land
Where cannibals cut out of brown paper
In cardboard jungles feast and caper,
Where the sea's sharp waves continually
Waver against the shore faithfully
And the yellow sun above is thin and flat
With a collar of black spikes and spines
To tell the innocent childish heart that
It shines
And warms (see where she stands and stammers)
The dear fat mother of the Katzenjammers.
Oh, for years and years she has stood
At the window and kept fairly good
Guard over the fat pies that she bakes
For her two children, those dancing heartaches.
Oh, the blue skies of that funny paper weather!
The distant birds like two eyebrows close together!
And the rustling paper roar
Of the waves
Against the paper sands of the paper shore!

❖

The Gramophone

Upon the lake
At Gramophone
A beastly bird
Sits on the bank
And dips its beak
Of sharpened bone
Into a haunted
Tank
That ripples with an eternal stone.

When the ladies descend the stairs,
Some eat their fans
And others comb their hair.
But Miss Mumblecrust
Picks up that beastly bird
And dips its beak
Into that round lake
That ripples with eternal stone
And dips its beak of sharpened bone
Into a pool of a young man singing
"I'm all alone
By the telephone!"

❖

The Death of the Poet

Above me the sun is hanging
From a tree.
Heavy the sun
Dragging down the branch.
My heart hangs heavy
The only leaf
Upon a red tree.
Heavy the heart that
Will not fall loose when
Autumn comes
But bring tree, bough and branch
To a gray bed.

When the stars stare
With yellow eyes
From their dark high chairs
Placed at the top
Of a black stairs
When the night is

Brown and black
Like Congou tea
Then the sunflowers
And other flowers
Touch the ground
And strive to see
Through the earth
To the sun.

When they open my grave
To steal my watch and ring
I'll not be there
But gone burrowing
For the sun
That hangs heavy
Dragging down the protesting branch
Bough and branch.
The sun that is my heart
The only leaf
Upon a red tree
Heavyheavyheavyheavy
To a gray grave.

❖

The Birth of Venus

I

In and underneath
The warm sea breathing
Up and down
Feverish-breasted with waves
White legs of papier-mâché assemble.
A torso of pink rubber
Has holes for long wooden arms
A wool and marble head
And room for the giant lover
Expectant upon the peacock-spotted marble shore.

II

Apples fall like desultory tennis
In the dark orchard where chaste stout trees
Stiffly fondle fondly
Whose roots flow like purple brooks
Over the ground-hog hollow earth.
We lie so close
Upon the grass
The gunpowder in our thick-twigged hearts
Dreams of the fiercest command
So that our two hearts rush out
Like two red star-shells bursting from
The toothless mouths of cannon
Killing each other instantly
Among the demisemiquaver cricket cries
In the hush between the falls of pears
Like moons and stars in a green sky
Appear upon a green-needled lawn.
And sad old trees with bellies
Watch us
Until there is only one shadow between us
Until we have swallowed each other's
Fish-eyed soul
Until the red hair and branches
That lace and lightning the night
Of our limbs
Inmeshes entangles
Inextricably
In one explosive
Fated glow
While we lie in each other
Like one river
Drowning face down
In another river.

III

In the brown darkness
Of the earth beneath us
Lies the dead groundhog
Who died in bed.
Here in the starless fog
The subterranean branches
Of the ancient orchard
Wage battle
For night-soil and corpses.
These skull-sized apples
Mean the late-discovered shroud
Of the murthered child
Transformed into a hundred
Red gouts and gobbets
Of yellow wood and red blood.
So beneath our counterpane
Country of march-pane joy
Lie hate and death, battle
And conflicting rusty saws and
Orange-speckled swords.
From this love
The death of death
Up seventy gray stairs
Runs the eager messenger
To hang out
The very red eye of death again itself.

❖

Antichrist as a Child

When Antichrist was a child
He caught himself tracing
The capital letter A
On a window sill

And wondered why
Because his name contained no A.
And as he crookedly stood
In his mother's flower-garden
He wondered why she looked so sadly
Out of an upstairs window at him.
He wondered why his father stared so
Whenever he saw his little son
Walking in his soot-coloured suit.
He wondered why the flowers
And even the ugliest weeds
Avoided his fingers and his touch.
And when his shoes began to hurt
Because his feet were becoming hooves
He did not let on to anyone
For fear they would shoot him for a monster.
He wondered why he more and more
Dreamed of eclipses of the sun,
Of sunsets, ruined towns and zeppelins,
And especially inverted, upside down churches.

❖

Rewards for Ambitious Trees

Fame to trees may come
Through at last advancing
On the savage dunce
Who counts the syllables of time
In the castle near Dunsinane.
Some achieve the wearing of a young lady
Who is pursued in her farthingale
By a hot rash ravisher.
She clings like a pink wrist-watch
Imploring one to be hollow.

Some are very old
Or are planted by Bismarck
Or caught Wordsworth's eye.
Victory falls to those
That fall on people
Or kill a longhaired prince.
Some prophesy with wooden scream
The wicked farmer's death
The sunk sun
The fallen star
The rumpled nebulae. . . .

❖

The Dead Rainbow

PART TWO

Slow against the dead rainbow
Of the vertebrate street
That flows past my window
Her sullen feet grate
As if Death knocked a rusty nail
Into her coffin
Through her heart
That's soft as a muffin.
In her room she will die
On her hard bed
Lit by a square sigh
Of dead sky.
She will perish unwed
Unringed and unravished.
And outside the winds neigh
To rush her dust away
In a shape like an eel
Or a rotting automobile
And let her down
Into that scrotal town

Ever threatened by red crowds
Of heart-shaped clouds
That in the myrrh-breathed weather
Entwine fast together
And let down vines to raise
From the dust
The roars and brays
Of asses and lions
That hide
In that unremembered weather of the loins.
There she will lie until
Two hearts will
Beat upon the window-pane
Of her dust-drenched brain
The breath and infection
Of Lust's resurrection
That but ends in the graveyard's harvest
Of stooks and sheaves of stone
Buoys to mark the place where rest
In a wooden submarine
Sunk in the grave's latrine
White dead sailors sparsely carved from bone.

❖

Platonic Love

My love, I've watched you
All this summer afternoon I've watched you
Lying in the field in the sun
A pink heap of cloth and flesh in the grass
Your hat beside you was half full of berries
Which you must have picked where I am standing.
Then you turned lazy and lay down
In the summer sun and I came
Through the dark thick woods

To the edge of your field where I leaned
Against this fence post in the brambles.
The shadows of the trees flowed down to you
But I couldn't, although my shadow did.
It almost touched you before you left,
Almost, – until you looked up and saw
The black tide of shade coming at you
And walked home through brighter fields.

I did not dare come down to you because
I loved you, the shoddiest reason of all.
But now that you have gone, of course,
I run down the field to where you lay.
I stand and lie beside and walk around
The grass where you have slept.
That grass is all bent where you were, you know
And different. It will still be different
Months from now and makes a green lady,
A green gingerbread man of pressed down grass;
A flat green girl of bent shiny hay
Is all that lies where you have been.
What were you thinking of?
Oh God, this is all I'll have of you,
This is the nearest we shall be
As I lie beside this green thin phantom.
This green ghost where you have lain
Shall whirl with me down
And down, until I die,
Down and down the wells and passageways of Time.
Light as newspaper floating on the streets
This my green hollow love.

Come sit on my knee, green emptiness
Here's a kiss for you, puff-of-air.
Come into my bed, green miss,
Green marionette, and I will be
Monsieur Ventriloquist
Forcing you to say you love me
And all too easily making you say it.

What light green arms you have, my dear.
What lovely light and green limbs
And your face! And your green flowing hair!
If I leave you here in this field
I know where to find you
Even when you've faded away in the rain
And are covered with snow, even
Next year I shall be able to dig you up,
Green Girl.
But God I am sick of watching where Love lies
And sick of shadow-girls
Kissing shadow-guys.

✤

The Tall Black Hat

As a child, I dreamt of tomorrow
Of the word "tomorrow" itself.
The word was a man in a tall black hat
Who walked in black clothes through
Green fields of quiet rain that
Beneath gray cloudfields grew.

Tall as trees or Abraham Lincoln
Were that man's brothers
Who when they become To-day
Die and dissolve one by one
Like licorice morning shadows
When held in the mouth of the sun.

Yesterday is an old greataunt
Rocked off in her rocking chair
To cellars where old light and snow
And all yesterdays go;

To-day was a small girl bringing
China cupfuls of water and air
And cages of robins singing,
"It is positively no crime
To have pleasure in Present Time."

But Tomorrow is most impressive
Like the hired man back from the fair
He comes to the child still sleeping
With pockets of longer hair,
A handful of longer fingers
And the Indian I remember
At dusk, crossing Market Square.

The man in the tall black hat
Brought the gipsy who was drunk
And the white faced cat
Who stepped before my stepmother
The very first time she came.

He gave the child a yellow leaf,
He holds the arrow for my heart,
He dropped the playing card in the lane,
He brought the dancing weasel,
And the old man playing the jewsharp.

He brings the wind and the sun
And the stalks of dead teazle
Seen on a windless winter walk,
He fetches a journey's direction
From his garden of weathervanes
And mines, like diamonds, the tears
For the glittering windowpanes
Of rain and sorrow.

All the days of all the years
The dark provider hunts me
Whom I named Sir Thomas Tomorrow
After my dream of him,

And in the grave fields of mystery
This black man has brothers
Who have followed him and come
Ever since with all I must see,
With Earth, Heaven and the tenor drum
I played in the C.O.T.C.,
The sound of bells and stars in a tree
Are stuck to their thumb
And lie in their tall black hats and pockets
Like pictures in locked and closed lockets.

At midnight he knocked and arrived
As the old woman really rocked away
And he took off his tall hat which
Changed into a small white cup,
White as the new light of day.
To the girl as small as a switch,
The girl who wakes me up,
His tallness and blackness shrank
To leave behind on the floor
From his pockets of come to pass
Puzzles and lonely birds to see
Diamonded names upon window glass,
A whistle, a straw and a tree.

But see out where small in the dawn
Through the hanging wingflash dance
Of the little flies, the wrens and the doves
Who are the seconds and minutes and hours
Floating over the acres of distance,
See his brother with feet of slate
Begin to walk through the wet flowers
Towards me with his speck of Future
And a tall black hatful of Fate.

The Horn

What is the horn that the dawn holds,
A soft shrill horn of feathers,
Cold as the dew on the grass by the paths,
Warm as the fire in the match in the box.
When this horn blows, in a sky of the sun
There rises our green star of earth
And the four evangelists who've borne
Thy bed down through the night
Now leave thee still thine eyes to see
The sun's separation of shadows.

Neither capons nor pullets nor hens
Can wake the sun and the world;
Only the prophets of the Old Testament
Huge old cocks, all speckled and barred,
Their wings like ragged pages of sermons,
Only they from their roosts in the henhouse
Can rouse the bread from its oven-sleep,
Raise the smoke from the haunted chimney.

Fierce old cock whose eyes look blind
So glaring and inspired are they,
Who live in this dungeon of cramp and dirt;
Fierce old fowl with shaking red wattles
Surrounding a beak like a kernel of wheat,
A yellow beak, plump, twisted and sharp
Which opens, hinged and prizing cry,
To show the sun's fistful of golden darts.

From *February Eclogue:*
Branwell's Sestina

My love I give to you a threefold thing,
A jewsharp serenade, a song I've made
And a sparkling pretty rose diamond ring.
To haste your love to me by fate delayed.
Zing zing zing zing, azeezing, azeezing,
Azuggazing, azeezug–zug–azing.

Six reasons are there for my loving you :
Your eyes, voice, beak, legs, mind and feathers white;
Feathers like snow, like cloud, like milk, like salt,
White white against the green grass in the spring.
Oh white angel in bethlehems of grime
Teach my slow wits to understand your worth.

With only reckless hope, not the true worth
That should raise up a suitor wooing you,
I try to know that stainless mind, so white
That crystal shafts and lily mines of salt
Seem when compared coal black : and in love's spring
I beg forgiveness for my own mind's grime.

Your paddling legs do even cleanse that grime;
When I scan all your parts and all your worth,
Sometimes they seem the prettiest part of you,
Those orange sticks beneath your body white,
Those sturdy swimming oars that somersault
Above your body at the pond in spring.

When your swift beak dives down for frog offspring,
Oh resting in his bathos hut of muddy grime
How sweet to be a frog that's nothing worth
Lifted to the sublime up up by you
By your fox orange beak and neck so white,
Your beak so bright it hurts the eye like salt.

Venison needs a humble pinch of salt;
You need the sounds that from your beak do spring,
Bragful when your feet feel spring's first thaw-grime,
Stout and most vigorous and strong when worth
We argue among us; rasping when you
See robbers in the yard with moonlight white.

But most I love – that's neither orange nor white –
Your circular blue eyes intense as salt :
They shot and caught my blizzardheart for spring,
First sky they cracked into my egg of grime,
First rain they let from out your storms of worth.
For these six things then I praise and love you
And now I beg you, my dread goddess white,
To slake my dry salt lips with mercy's spring
And touch my cold grime with your golden worth.

May Eclogue

❖ ❖ ❖

ARGUMENT

> *Effie and Fanny are discovered drynursing the entire flock of goslings. Fanny describes how two propagandists recently roaming the backwoods have met an interesting fate.*

❖ ❖ ❖

EFFIE FANNY

I think that yours will turn out white
    And mine will be the gray ones
But all just now are furry bright
    Like infant furry pocket suns.

Goslings now, goslings all
Run not near the muskrat's hall
Dancing weasel might prance up.

Yours will be white, mine will be gray,
   Some day now in the future,
But neither goose nor gander they
   Now play in tender nurture.

Goslings there, goslings dear
Swim not to those rushes near
Waiting skunk might on you sup.

Pray what's the news of snapping turtles
   And what of snapping foxes
We fend, we guard, we watch for rascals
   That snatch our goslings from us.

FANNY

To be worse for I heard from a cousin
   Who was down here loading caddises & cressing
That two strange geese of the scientific variety
     Had preached all year for their society,
   You do know how big the families are back there,
Forty-two or fifty-two goslings is not a thing rare.
     The section is so overpopulated,
   It puffs up and over with children inflated.
These two ladies want to save all the hill country women
     From all that labour and child-labouring.
 "I've got the greatest news for you," they juicy say,
To some farm wife who looks like a big five ring circus **tent**
     Held down by small children holding on it.
 "We can show you how to stop this torment to-day,
We can show you how to stop conceiving & bearing
     children."
   They open up their big black boxes then :
 "This piece of straw, this frazzled bit of string, this old
Button from a castrati's overcoat at his death sold,
     Worth twenty babes any day and all free !"
 Well, some places they caused a riot jamboree,
And some other places the people didn't catch on what
     They meant. "To bring forth children never not –
   Who now could want that desert barren state?" they said.

"But you could have one or plan for two, plump & decent fed
    And warmly clothed," these smooth ladies rejoined.
"You then could buy yourself a kill-yourself-if-you-touch-it
    And a watch-everybody-squeeze-up-from-hell-while-you-sit;
    An electric jelly-fish warmer than a husband to go to bed
        with you
    And a pass-like-a-vulture-shadow and get your sons to do
    Two-backed tricks in the back and flatten 5,000,000 frogs
        too."
        "But," said the people, "we like having more, once
            joined;
        And one doesn't raise as well as a dozen and a half.
        You grow us more food and wages, smarty;
        Meanwhile we'll keep hoeing our own kindergarty.
Just how could one huge cow rest its heart on one little calf?
        Children are our life, our bread and our clothing,
        With their two little arms & legs & their one head
    They come toppling shouting out of us to prove we're not
        dead.
        Can God not damn you for hating being?"
    Now then the two biddies came to the conclusion
After a year of very little success that pretty soon
        They'd have to go back when one night they met
        Coming up a hill toward them two handsome yet
Sort of grim rakish sly curly young men who looked just
        like.
    "Why you slick ladies aren't going farther
    In this wet and no-dry-hotel-for-miles weather?"
"We can suffer far more than this for the cause of no-tyke.
        The more it rains on us, the more we laugh,
    It can't wet us with what we waxy know; we scoff
At rain and suffer to decrease humanity : we're glad
To outwit any fertility." The two brothers bade
        Them come for food & shelter to their house.
    They went, more than slightly attracted, to this place.
It was old, mossy roofed & gabled with many windows
        Set between leafy thick appletree rows.
    The brothers asked these expert girls to be their wives.
First these spinsters said not by the beard of their chinny
        lives.

At length to a ceaseless mad tattooing
Of caresses they allowed the brothers' wooing
And made their special preparations for the bridal night.
    They tied the brothers up in sheets of tight
  Glass, beaten gold, cork, rubber, netting, stoppers, sand;
They themselves dammed their wombs with a pretty
      skilful hand
    And lay back waiting for the sensation
Of an interesting lively copulation,
Without any of the disfiguring after effects necessary for
      population.
    Nevertheless and oh nevertheless
  The brothers so handled their part of the process
That in six weeks' time the ladies in question were with
      child,
    Seeded down by those strange men dark & wild.
"How on earth did you do this to us, Roderick?"
They groaned & shrieked & roared. "And you too, dreadful
      Benedict!"
    "Madams, we are twins," the brothers explained,
"And for centuries our old family has gained
New members for itself always in twos or threes or fours.
    Our emblem is a white sow with twelve pigs
  All sucking her dry, like bishops in periwigs
All translating at a Holy Bible, and *you* we picked
    To test our fertile power on since you kicked
Our family's sense of lively birth in the teeth.
From this day may you billow saw waddle gag groan
      beneath
    The ripeness of a Nile in bringing forth!"
A dark cloud swept thunderously down from the North
Of snapping turtles, newts & hopping toads; as in a dream
    The women's loins poured forth a swollen stream
Until the brothers moved them to their granary
Where they were turned into strong & sturdy machinery;
    One into a large & squat fanning mill,
  The other to a tall conical cylindrical
Iron Maiden used for threshing seeds from ripe sunflowers.
So usefully did end the lives of those insistent life devourers.

From September Eclogue:
Drunken Preacher's Sermon

Lo, it was the last supper, I leader from gutter
Tell you tall and short tinkery folks gathered.
What did those white souls eat while their Lord talked :
I don't know indeed I don't, maybe sandwiches.
And He said haughtily head up to the twelve,
"I'll ask you assafoetidae again I will,
   Isn't there one, one disciple with the spunk to betray me ?"
They all fumbled their food, fed themselves slowly.
"Otherwise you see all my work ought in value is."
"I will," quavered weakly woefully poor Judas,
   Runty little redhaired man runaway parents from him.
"I'll go through with ghoulish Holy Ghost necessary job."
Even then at the end of it elder tree saw he.
His death, his Lord's death held him at Lord's supper.
So you've all certainly betrayed him so you've done
Something for him by my bottle faith fiddle de dee you
      have.

❖

From October Eclogue:
Raymond's Autumn Song

This song is like the grapes now
   Black in the arbours of fences,
Wild apples from their lane bough
   Savage and sweet to the senses.

Nailed and studded are the quietnesses
   With wrinkled dark butternuts,
Prickly beechnuts of brown darknesses,
   Ripe burs' pinch and hook and clutch.

The shorter sun sets farther south,
   The foxes are about now,
The wind whistles with a narrow mouth,
Up to the gooseshed we had better go.

November Eclogue

❖ ❖ ❖

ARGUMENT
Four birds discuss the calendar.

❖ ❖ ❖

OOKPIK STARLING WILDGOOSE MOPSUS

Birdies, can there be any doubt
My master, Winter, turns the wheel,
   The Miller whom none love.
I at the spindle pole have been
And through the swarming shuddering snow
   Seen at work the God of Death;
Winter and Death turn all the world,
Man and continents come apart
   Like skin from flesh from bone.
The world was planned in cold arithmetic,
Numbers flapping like vultures fast & thick
Down and around my merry Master Zero
Like birds of prey about a stone dead hero.

STARLING

The year begins when it grows warm;
Then I once more do mate and chirp
   And fly out from the town.
It is not year or time at all
When all there's eatable is dung
   And all is frozen round.
Give me the eaves of a steam laundry
Where I dream of upperworld spring
   About this grave of cold.
Once I lived in a place of sun,
I wish I knew how there to run,
Migrationless I debris am
Yet know the world begins with warm.

WILDGOOSE

My wings tell me that September*
Shall the year's beginning be;
   Up those wide rungs I climb
And fly a vigorous sabbath south
And find no winter in my year
But live a summer seesaw;
Two summers like a figure eight
Two wings like tables of the law
   Are my four seasons.
The wobbling earth with its Goliath snows
I steady and defeat with feathered blows.
The year begins when death and chaos sprout
And I must with a new world beat them out.

MOPSUS

A sun, a moon, a crowd of stars,
A calendar nor clock is he
   By whom I start my year.
He is most like a sun for he
Makes his beholders into suns,
   Shadowless and timeless.
At the winter sunstill some say
He dared be born; on darkest day
   A babe of seven hours
He crushed the four proud and great directions
Into the four corners of his small cradle.
He made it what time of year he pleased, changed
Snow into grass and gave to all such powers.

* The Jews begin their year in September.

Rachel

When I was a young young man
   In passing the city dump
Out of smoking rubbish I heard
   A small and rusty wail :

Naked without any clothes
   Unwashed from the caul
   Thy navel string uncut
A crusted, besmattered and loathsome thing.

I ruined my clothes and stank for a week
   But I brought you to my house.
I found that your mother was a gipsy
   Your father an Indian.

Live, I said, and you lived.
   You grew like a flax field
Your hair gold as the Sun
   Your breasts were blossoms.

I passed your foster house,
   It was the time of love.
I rewarded your music teacher
   For the pearly runs in your Scarlatti

It was the time of love.
I was so afraid you might say no.
   My heart beat like giant steps
   I felt agony in your garden.

Then you came to my house.
I was ashamed to ask you so often.
   I gave you a golden ring
   I gave you a glass pen.

   You dressed in silk
   You bathed in milk
But on your shoulder as we
Embraced I saw the red speck.

It had never washed off
   But I went unto you
   With all the more love :
You prospered into a kingdom.

I must go away to abroad :
   When I returned uptown
I met you and you knew me not,
   Your hair like flax tow

   Crimped like an eggbeater, your
Mouth like a cannibal's – bloody,
Your eyelids – massive with blue mud;
   And a handmuff made of bats' fur.

I found out about your carryings on,
   Your lovers and infidelities.
My child you had sold to a brothel,
   You had to pay for your men.

In pity I bribed men to go to you,
   But your two biggest lovers,
Lord Dragon and Count Dino,
   I whispered your triple crossings.

They gathered their devils and mobs.
In the name of virtue they attacked
   Your tall town house :
You bore then your seven month bastard.

They brought you out on your balcony,
   Your house devoured with flame,
   Out they threw you and the dogs
      Licked your blood up.

Then from your hand I took
   My ring : from the hag's claw
   I took my golden ring,
Her breasts like pigsties.

I found her child and I
Washed you in my tears.
Still there is the spot
Red on your shoulder – a speck.

I wash you with my tears
And still the speck remains,
My darling, it is my fault –
I have not tears enough.

❖

Doomsday, or the Redheaded Woodpecker

Red Sky
Morning
Shaking like a scarlet head
Doomsday
Rise Up
Spring your lids, you dead

Scrape out
Coffins
Put yourself together
Pat that dust
Find that bust
This is the last weather

Trumpet
Drummer
Thunder
Vomit you cannibals
Shake out those
Those old flesh dresses
For the resurrection parties and balls.

Here comes St. Sebastian with a handful
Of arrows
The big threshing woodpecker is
Beating on the green drum
Here comes the poor boy who got caught in
The harrows
Here comes St. Bartholemew with his skin :
Scroll away
Hell this way
Heaven that
Rat a tat tat
There goes Death and there goes Sin
Here come Cain and Abel
Hand in hand
Here come horizontals turning into slopes.
Here comes a table
Changing back to a tree and
Here come the hanged people skipping
With their ropes.

Red sky
Morning
Shaking like a scarlet head
Doomsday!
Rise up!
Spring your lids, you dead!
Scrape out
Coffins!
Put yourself together!
Pat that dust
Find that bust
This the last weather!

Trumpet!
Drummer!
Thunder!
Vomit you cannibals!
Shake out those,
Those old flesh dresses
For the resurrection parties and balls!

Le Tombeau de Pierre Falcon

Pierre Falcon,
You say here along with this unsingable music
That on June nineteenth these Burnt Wood people
Ah yes, the Métis were dark, so called Bois-Brûlés,
Arrived near this settlement of Lord Selkirk's
Fort Douglas

You say in this second verse that your Burnt Woods
Took three foreigners prisoner at Frog Plain.
These foreigners were Scotchmen from the Orkneys
Who had come, as you put it, to rob your – Pierre
    Falcon's –
Country.

Well we were just about to unhorse
When we heard two of us give, give voice.
Two of our men cried, "Hey! Look back, look back!
    The Anglo-Sack
    Coming for to attack."

Right away smartly we veered about
Galloping at them with a shout!
You know we did trap all, all those Grenadiers!
    They could not move
    Those horseless cavaliers.

Now we like honourable men did act,
Sent an ambassador – yes, in fact!
"Monsieur Governor! Would you like to stay?
    A moment spare –
    There's something we'd like to say."

Governor, Governor, full of ire.
"Soldiers!" he cries, "Fire! Fire!"
So they fire the first and their muskets roar!
    They almost kill
    Our ambassador!

Governor thought himself a king.
He wished an iron rod to swing.
Like a lofty lord he tries to act.
      Bad luck, old chap!
      A bit too hard you whacked!

When we went galloping, galloping by
Governor thought that he would try
For to chase and frighten us Bois-Brûlés.
      Catastrophe!
      Dead on the ground he lay.

Dead on the ground lots of grenadiers too.
Plenty of grenadiers, a whole slew.
We've almost stamped out his whole army
      Of so many
      Five or four left there be.

You should have seen those Englishmen –
Bois-Brûlés chasing them, chasing them.
From bluff to bluff they stumbled that day
      While the Bois-Brûlés
      Shouted "Hurray!"

And now in this eleventh verse you ask
Who made up this song and then you tell us
That you yourself made it up – Pierre Falcon.
You made it up to sing the glory of the
Burnt Wood People.

Far away and dear, spunky old and early poet
I wish I could sing the praises of the Neon People
To You.

P. K. PAGE

Patricia Page was born in England in 1917, but moved to Canada as a young child. She attended St Hilda's School in Calgary and during the war was associated with the Montreal little magazine *Preview*. In 1950 she married W. A. Irwin, then with the National Film Board, but later abroad with the Department of External Affairs. Her two books of poetry are *As Ten as Twenty* (The Ryerson Press, 1946) and *The Metal and the Flower* (McClelland and Stewart Limited, 1954). She has published practically no poetry since 1954, but has suggested that the pen and crayon drawings of recent years are a kind of continuation of her writing. "It's the same pen." Some of these are reproduced in *Tamarack Review* (Summer, 1960).

Stories of Snow

Those in the vegetable rain retain
an area behind their sprouting eyes
held soft and rounded with the dream of snow
precious and reminiscent as those globes –
souvenir of some never nether land –
which hold their snow storms circular, complete,
high in a tall and teakwood cabinet.

In countries where the leaves are large as hands
where flowers protrude their fleshy chins
and call their colours
an imaginary snow storm sometimes falls
among the lilies.
And in the early morning one will waken
to think the glowing linen of his pillow
a northern drift, will find himself mistaken
and lie back weeping.
And there the story shifts from head to head,
of how, in Holland, from their feather beds
hunters arise and part the flakes and go
forth to the frozen lakes in search of swans –
the snow light falling white along their guns,
their breath in plumes.
While tethered in the wind like sleeping gulls
ice boats wait the raising of their wings
to skim the electric ice at such a speed
they leap the jet strips of the naked water,
and how these flying, sailing hunters feel
air in their mouths as terrible as ether.
And on the story runs that even drinks
in that white landscape dare to be no colour;
how, flasked and water clear, the liquor slips
silver against the hunters' moving hips.

And of the swan in death these dreamers tell
of its last flight and how it falls, a plummet,
pierced by the freezing bullet

and how three feathers, loosened by the shot,
descend like snow upon it.
While hunters plunge their fingers in its down
deep as a drift, and dive their hands
up to the neck of the wrist
in that warm metamorphosis of snow
as gentle as the sort that woodsmen know
who, lost in the white circle, fall at last
and dream their way to death.

And stories of this kind are often told
in countries where great flowers bar the roads
with reds and blues which seal the route to snow –
as if, in telling, raconteurs unlock
the colour with its complement and go
through to the area behind the eyes
where silent, unrefractive whiteness lies.

Adolescence

In love they wore themselves in a green embrace.
A silken rain fell through the spring upon them.
In the park she fed the swans and he
whittled nervously with his strange hands.
And white was mixed with all their colours
as if they drew it from the flowering trees.

At night his two-finger whistle brought her down
the waterfall stairs to his shy smile
which, like an eddy, turned her round and round
lazily and slowly so her will
was nowhere – as in dreams things are and aren't.

Walking along the avenues in the dark
street lamps sang like sopranos in their heads
with a violence they never understood
and all their movements when they were together
had no conclusion.

Only leaning into the question had they motion :
after they parted were savage and swift as gulls.
Asking and asking the hostile emptiness
they were as sharp as partly sculptured stone
and all who watched, forgetting, were amazed
to see them form and fade before their eyes.

✤

The Stenographers

After the brief bivouac of Sunday,
their eyes, in the forced march of Monday to Saturday,
hoist the white flag, flutter in the snow storm of paper,
haul it down and crack in the midsun of temper.

In the pause between the first draft and the carbon
they glimpse the smooth hours when they were children –
the ride in the ice-cart, the ice-man's name,
the end of the route and the long walk home;

remember the sea where floats at high tide
were sea marrows growing on the scatter-green vine
or spools of grey toffee, or wasps' nests on water;
remember the sand and the leaves of the country.

Bell rings and they go and the voice draws their pencil
like a sled across snow; when its runners are frozen
rope snaps and the voice then is pulling no burden
but runs like a dog on the winter of paper.

Their climates are winter and summer – no wind
for the kites of their hearts – no wind for a flight;
a breeze at the most, to tumble them over
and leave them like rubbish – the boy-friends of blood.

In the inch of the noon as they move they are stagnant.
The terrible calm of the noon is their anguish;
the lip of the counter, the shapes of the straws
like icicles breaking their tongues are invaders.

Their beds are their oceans – salt water of weeping
the waves that they know – the tide before sleep;
and fighting to drown they assemble their sheep
in columns and watch them leap desks for their fences
and stare at them with their own mirror-worn faces.

In the felt of the morning the calico minded,
sufficiently starched, insert papers, hit keys,
efficient and sure as their adding machines;
yet they weep in the vault, they are taut as net curtains
stretched upon frames. In their eyes I have seen
the pin men of madness in marathon trim
race round the track of the stadium pupil.

The Bands and the Beautiful Children

Band makes a tunnel of the open street
at first, hearing it;
seeing it, band becomes
high; brasses ascending on the strings of sun
build their own auditorium of light,
windows from cornets
and a dome of drums.

And always attendant on bands, the beautiful children,
white with running and innocence;
and the arthritic old
who, patient behind their windows
are no longer split by the quick yellow of imagination
or carried beyond their angular limits of distance.

But the children move
in the trembling building of sound,
sure as a choir
until band breaks and scatters,
crumbles about them and is made of men
tired and grumbling
on the straggling grass.

And the children, lost, lost,
in an open space,
remember the certainty of the anchored home
and cry on the unknown edge of their own city
their lips stiff from an imaginary trumpet.

❖

Photos of a Salt Mine

How innocent their lives look,
how like a child's
dream of caves and winter, both combined :
the steep descent to whiteness
and the stope
with its striated walls
their folds all leaning as if pointing to
the greater whiteness still,
that great white bank
with its decisive front,
that seam upon a slope,
salt's lovely ice.

And wonderful underfoot the snow of salt,
the fine
particles a broom could sweep,
one thinks
muckers might make angels in its drifts,
as children do in snow,
lovers in sheets,
lie down and leave imprinted where they lay
a feathered creature holier than they.

And in the outworked stopes
with lamps and ropes
up miniature matterhorns
the miners climb,
probe with their lights
the ancient folds of rock –
syncline and anticline –
and scoop from darkness an aladdin's cave :
rubies and opals glitter from its walls.

But hoses douse the brilliance of these jewels,
melt fire to brine.
Salt's bitter water trickles thin and forms
slow fathoms down
a lake within a cave
lacquered with jet –
white's opposite.
There grey on black the boating miners float
to mend the stays and struts of that old stope
and deeply underground
their words resound,
are multiplied by echo, swell and grow
and make a climate of a miner's voice.

So all the photographs like children's wishes
are filled with caves or winter,
innocence
has acted as a filter,
selected only beauty from the mine.

Except in the last picture,
it is shot
from an acute high angle. In a pit
figures the size of pins are strangely lit
and might be dancing but you know they're not.
Like Dante's vision of the nether hell
men struggle with the bright cold fires of salt
locked in the black inferno of the rock :
the filter here, not innocence but guilt.

T-Bar

Relentless, black on white, the cable runs
through metal arches up the mountainside.
At intervals giant pickaxes are hung
on long hydraulic springs. The skiers ride
propped by the axehead, twin automatons
supported by its handle, one each side.

In twos they move slow motion up the steep
incision in the mountain. Climb. Climb.
Somnambulists, bolt upright in their sleep
their phantom poles swung lazily behind,
while to the right, the empty T-bars keep
in mute descent, slow monstrous jigging time.

Captive the skiers now and innocent,
wards of eternity, each pair alone.
They mount the easy vertical ascent,
pass through successive arches, bride and groom,
as through successive naves, are newly wed
participants in some recurring dream.

So do they move forever. Clocks are broken.
In zones of silence they grow tall and slow,
inanimate dreamers, mild and gentle-spoken,
blood brothers of the haemophilic snow
until the summit breaks and they awaken
imagos from the stricture of the tow.

Jerked from her chrysalis the sleeping bride
suffers too sudden freedom like a pain.
The dreaming bridegroom severed from her side
singles her out, the old wound aches again.
Uncertain, lost, upon a wintry height
these two not separate yet no longer one.

But clocks begin to peck and sing. The slow
extended minute like a rubber band
snaps back to nothing and the skiers go
quickly articulate, while far behind
etching the sky-line, obdurate and slow
the spastic T-bars pivot and descend.

❖

Sisters

These children split each other open like nuts,
break and crack in the small house,
are doors slamming.
Still, on the whole, are gentle for mother, take
her simple comfort like a drink of milk.

Fierce on the street they own the sun and spin
on separate axes
attract about them in their motion all
the shrieking neighbourhood of little earths;
in violence hold hatred in their mouths.

With evening their joint gentle laughter leads
them into pastures of each others eyes;
beyond, the world is barren; they contract
tenderness from each other like disease
and talk as if each word had just been born –
a butterfly, and soft from its cocoon.

❖

Young Girls

Nothing, not even fear of punishment
can stop the giggle in a girl.
Oh mothers' trim
shapes on the chesterfield cannot dispel
their lolloping fatness.
Adolescence tumbles about in them
on the cinder schoolyard or behind the expensive gates.

See them in class like porpoises
with smiles and tears
loosed from the same subterranean faucet; some
find individual adventure in
the obtuse angle, some in a phrase
that leaps like a smaller fish from a sea of words.
But most, deep in their daze, dawdle and roll;
their little breasts like wounds beneath their clothes.

A shoal of them in a room makes it a pool.
How can one teacher keep the water out,
or, being adult, find the springs and taps
of their tempers and tortures?
Who, on a field filled with their female cries
can reel them in on a line of words
or land them neatly in a net?
On the dry ground they goggle, flounder, flap.

Too much weeping in them and unfamiliar blood
has set them perilously afloat.
Not divers these – but as if the water rose up in a flood
making them partially amphibious
and always drowning a little and hearing bells;
until the day the shore line wavers less,
and caught and swung on the bright hooks of their sex,
   earth becomes home – their natural element.

❖

Intractable Between Them
Grows ...

Intractable between them grows
a garden of barbed wire and roses.
Burning briars like flames devour
their too innocent attire.
Dare they meet, the blackened wire
tears the intervening air.

Trespassers have wandered through
texture of flesh and petals.
Dogs like arrows moved along
pathways that their noses knew.
While the two who laid it out
find the metal and the flower
fatal underfoot.

Black and white at midnight glows
this garden of barbed wire and roses.
Doused with darkness roses burn
coolly as a rainy moon;
beneath a rainy moon or none
silver the sheath on barb and thorn.

Change the garden, scale and plan;
wall it, make it annual.
There the briary flower grew.
There the brambled wire ran.
While they sleep the garden grows,
deepest wish annuls the will :
perfect still the wire and rose.

❖

Portrait of Marina

Far out the sea has never moved. It is
prussian forever, rough as teazled wool
some antique skipper worked into a frame
to bear his lost four-master.
                                    Where it hangs
now in a sunny parlour, none recalls
how all his stitches, interspersed with oaths
had made his one pale spinster daughter grow
transparent with migraines – and how his call
fretted her more than waves.
                                    Her name
Marina, for his youthful wish –
boomed at the font of that small salty church
where sailors lurched like drunkards, would, he felt
make her a water woman, rich with bells.
To her, the name Marina simply meant
he held his furious needle for her thin
fingers to thread again with more blue wool
to sew the ocean of his memory.
Now, where the picture hangs, a dimity
young inland housewife with inherited
clocks under bells and ostrich eggs on shelves
pours amber tea in small rice china cups
and reconstructs

how great-great-grandpappa at ninety-three
his fingers knotted with arthritis, his
old eyes grown agatey with cataracts
became as docile as a child again –
that fearful salty man –
and sat, wrapped round in faded paisley shawls
gently embroidering.
While aunt Marina in grey worsted, warped
without a smack of salt, came to his call
the sole survivor of his last shipwreck.

    *   *   *

Slightly offshore, it glints. Each wave is capped
with broken mirrors. Like Marina's head
the glinting of these waves.
She walked forever antlered with migraines
her pain forever putting forth new shoots
until her strange unlovely head became
a kind of candelabra – delicate –
where all her tears were perilously hung
and caught the light as waves that catch the sun.
The salt upon the panes, the grains of sand
that crunched beneath her heel
her father's voice, "Marina!" – all these broke
her trembling edifice. The needle shook
like ice between her fingers.
In her head
too many mirrors dizzied her and broke.

    *   *   *

But where the wave breaks, where it rises green
turns into gelatine, becomes a glass
simply for seeing stones through, runs across
the coloured shells and pebbles of the shore
and makes an aspic of them
then sucks back
in foam and undertow –
this aspect of the sea
Marina never knew.

For her the sea was Father's Fearful Sea
harsh with sea serpents
winds and drowning men.
For her it held no spiral of a shell
for her descent to dreams,
it held no bells.
And where it moved in shallows it was more
imminently a danger, more alive
than where it lay off shore full fathom five.

❖

Probationer

Floats out of anaesthetic
helium hipped
a bird a bride your breath could bruise,
is blurred.

Re-forms in bright enamel, tiny, chips
into recurring selves
a hundred of her
giving you smiles and small white pills of water.

Grows in delirium as striped and strange
as any tiger crouching in the flowers.
Her metal finger tip
taps out your pulse.

Intrinsic to your pain
lives in its acre
and only there because your wound has made her,
beyond its radius she has never been.

Is sly and clever suddenly, creates
you wholly out of sheets and air – fullgrown.
Most wonderfully makes a halo of your hair.
Gives you a name – your own.

Oh, in the easy mornings comes with smiles,
tipping the window so it spills the sun
carries the basin plastic with slipping water
and calls it fun.

For she is only a girl. And crisis over
she is herself again – clumsy and gauche,
her jokes too hearty
and her touch too rough.

And by a slow dissolve
becomes at last,
someone you've always known –
yourself perhaps.

Yet alters when you leave. From her stiff starch
she overflows in laughs, is proud and shy
and as if you are a present she has made,
she gives you away.

❖

Arras

Consider a new habit – classical,
and trees espaliered on the wall like candelabra.
How still upon that lawn our sandalled feet.

But a peacock rattling its rattan tail and screaming
has found a point of entry. Through whose eye
did it insinuate in furled disguise
to shake its jewels and silk upon that grass?

The peaches hang like lanterns. No one joins
those figures on the arras.
                      Who am I
or who am I become that walking here
I am observer, other, Gemini,
starred for a green garden of cinema?

I ask, what did they deal me in this pack?
The cards, all suits, are royal when I look.
My fingers slipping on a monarch's face
twitch and go slack.
I want a hand to clutch, a heart to crack.

No one is moving now, the stillness is
infinite. If I should make a break. . . .
take to my springy heels . . . ? But nothing moves.
The spinning world is stuck upon its poles,
the stillness points a bone at me. I fear
the future on this arras.
                      I confess:
It was my eye.
Voluptuous it came.
Its head the ferrule and its lovely tail
folded so sweetly; it was strangely slim
to fit the retina. And then it shook
and was a peacock – living patina,
eye-bright – maculate!
Does no one care?

I thought their hands might hold me if I spoke.
I dreamed the bite of fingers in my flesh,
their poke smashed by an image, but they stand
as if within a treacle, motionless,
folding slow eyes on nothing. While they stare
another line has trolled the encircling air,
another bird assumes its furled disguise.

LEONARD
COHEN

Leonard Cohen was born in Montreal in 1934 and attended McGill University, where his first book, *Let Us Compare Mythologies* (1956, republished 1966), initiated the McGill Poetry Series. He is a skilful and evocative reader of his own work, sometimes accompanying himself on the guitar in Montreal nightclubs, on the CBC, and elsewhere. His second volume of poetry was *The Spice-Box of Earth* (1961) followed in 1964 by *Flowers for Hitler*. His novels are *The Favourite Game* (1963) and *Beautiful Losers* (1966). His latest collection of poems is *Parasites of Heaven* (1966). Mr. Cohen's publisher is McClelland and Stewart Limited.

A Kite is a Victim

A kite is a victim you are sure of.
You love it because it pulls
gentle enough to call you master,
strong enough to call you fool;
because it lives
like a desperate trained falcon
in the high sweet air,
and you can always haul it down
to tame it in your drawer.

A kite is a fish you have already caught
in a pool where no fish come,
so you play him carefully and long,
and hope he won't give up,
or the wind die down.

A kite is the last poem you've written,
so you give it to the wind,
but you don't let it go
until someone finds you
something else to do.

A kite is a contract of glory
that must be made with the sun,
so you make friends with the field
the river and the wind,
then you pray the whole cold night before,
under the travelling cordless moon,
to make you worthy and lyric and pure.

Story

She tells me a child built her house
one Spring afternoon,
but that the child was killed
crossing the street.

She says she read it in the newspaper,
that at the corner of this and that avenue
a child was run down by an automobile.

Of course I do not believe her.
She has built the house herself,
hung the oranges and coloured beads in the doorways,
crayoned flowers on the walls.
She has made the paper things for the wind,
collected crooked stones for their shadows in the sun,
fastened yellow and dark balloons to the ceiling.

Each time I visit her
she repeats the story of the child to me,
I never question her. It is important
to understand one's part in a legend.

I take my place
among the paper fish and make-believe clocks,
naming the flowers she has drawn,
smiling while she paints my head on large clay coins,
and making a sort of courtly love to her
when she contemplates her own traffic death.

If It Were Spring

If it were Spring
       and I killed a man,
I would change him to leaves
and hang him from a tree,

a tree in a grove
       at the edge of a dune,
where small beasts came
to flee the sun.

Wind would make him
       part of song,
and rain would cling
like tiny crystal worlds

upon his branch
       of leaf-green skies,
and he would bear the dance
of fragile bone,

brush of wings
       against his maps of arteries,
and turn up a yellow-stomached flag
to herald the touring storm.

O my victim,
       you would grow your season
as I grew mine,
under the spell of growth,

an instrument
       of the blue sky,
an instrument of the sun,
a palm above the dark, splendid eyes.

What language the city will hear
       because of your death,
anguish explain,
sorrow relieve.

Everywhere I see
    the world waiting you,
the pens raised, walls prepared,
hands hung above the strings and keys.

And come Autumn
    I will spin a net
between your height and earth
to hold your crisp parts.

In the fields and orchards
    it must be turning Spring,
look at the faces
clustered around mine.

And I hear
    the irrefutable argument of hunger
whispered, spoken, shouted,
but never sung.

I will kill a man this week;
    before this week is gone
I will hang him to a tree,
I will see this mercy done.

❖

You All in White

Whatever cities are brought down,
I will always bring you poems,
and the fruit of orchards
I pass by.

Strangers in your bed,
excluded by our grief,
listening to sleep-whispering,
will hear their passion beautifully explained,
and weep because they cannot kiss
your distant face.

Lovers of my beloved,
watch how my words put on her lips like clothes,
how they wear her body like a rare shawl.
Fruit is pyramided on the window-sill,
songs flutter against the disappearing wall.

The sky of the city
Is washed in the fire
of Lebanese cedar and gold.
In smoky filigree cages
the apes and peacocks fret.
Now the cages do not hold,
in the burning street man and animal
perish in each other's arms,
peacocks drown around the melting throne.

Is it the king
who lies beside you listening?
Is it Solomon or David
or stuttering Charlemagne?
Is that his crown
in the suitcase beside your bed?

When we meet again,
you all in white,
I smelling of orchards,
when we meet –

But now you awaken,
and you are tired of this dream.
Turn toward the sad-eyed man.
He stayed by you all the night.
You will have something
to say to him.

Go By Brooks

Go by brooks, love,
Where fish stare,
Go by brooks,
I will pass there.

Go by rivers,
Where eels throng,
Rivers, love,
I won't be long.

Go by oceans,
Where whales sail,
Oceans, love,
I will not fail.

✤

As the Mist Leaves No Scar

As the mist leaves no scar
On the dark green hill,
So my body leaves no scar
On you, nor ever will.

When wind and hawk encounter,
What remains to keep?
So you and I encounter,
Then turn, then fall to sleep.

As many nights endure
Without a moon or star,
So will we endure
When one is gone and far.

Dead Song

As I lay dead
In my love-soaked bed,
Angels came to kiss my head.

I caught one gown
And wrestled her down
To be my girl in death town.

She will not fly.
She has promised to die.
What a clever corpse am I!

❖

For Anne

With Annie gone,
whose eyes to compare
With the morning sun?

Not that I did compare,
But I do compare
Now that she's gone.

Inquiry into the Nature
of Cruelty

A moth drowned in my urine,
his powdered body finally satin.
My eyes gleamed in the porcelain
like tiny dancing crematoria.

History is on my side, I pleaded,
as the drain drew circles in his wings.
(Had he not been bathed in urine
 I'd have rescued him to dry in the wind.)

❖

Sing to Fish,
Embrace the Beast

Sing to fish, embrace the beast,
But don't get up from the pond
With half your body a horse's body
Or wings from your backbone.
Sleep as a man beside the sleeping wolves
Without longing for a special sky
To darken and fur your hands.
Animals, do not kill for the human heart
Which under breasts of scale or flesh will cry.
O swallow, be a heart in the wind's high breast,
River the limbs of the sky with your singing blood
The dead are beginning to breathe:
I see my father splashing light like a jewel
In the swamp's black mud.

The Cuckold's Song

If this looks like a poem
I might as well warn you at the beginning
that it's not meant to be one.
I don't want to turn anything into poetry.
I know all about her part in it
but I'm not concerned with that right now.
This is between you and me.
Personally I don't give a damn who led who on:
in fact I wonder if I give a damn at all.
But a man's got to say something.
Anyhow you fed her 5 MacKewan Ales,
took her to your room, put the right records on,
and in an hour or two it was done.
I know all about passion and honour
but unfortunately this had really nothing to do with either:
oh there was passion I'm only too sure
and even a little honour
But the important thing was to cuckold Leonard Cohen.
Hell, I might just as well address this to the both of you:
I haven't time to write anything else.
I've got to say my prayers.
I've got to wait by the window.
I repeat: the important thing was to cuckold Leonard Cohen.
I like that line because it's got my name in it.
What really makes me sick
is that everything goes on as it went before:
I'm still a sort of friend,
I'm still a sort of lover.
But not for long:
that's why I'm telling this to the two of you.
The fact is I'm turning to gold, turning to gold.
It's a long process, they say,
it happens in stages.
This is to inform you that I've already turned to clay.

On the Sickness of My Love

Poems! break out!
break my head!
What good's a skull?
Help! help!
I need you!

She is getting old.
Her body tells her everything.
She has put aside cosmetics.
She is a prison of truth.

Make her get up!
dance the seven veils!
Poems! silence her body!
Make her friend of mirrors!

Do I have to put on my cape?
wander like the moon
over skies & skies of flesh
to depart again in the morning?

Can't I pretend
she grows prettier?
be a convict?
Can't my power fool me?
Can't I live in poems?

Hurry up! poems! lies!
Damn you weak music!
You've let arthritis in!
You're no poem,
you're a visa.

Last Dance at the Four Penny

Layton, when we dance our freilach
under the ghostly handkerchief,
the miracle rabbis of Prague and Vilna
resume their sawdust thrones,
and angels and men, asleep so long
in the cold palaces of disbelief,
gather in sausage-hung kitchens
to quarrel deliciously and debate
the sounds of the Ineffable Name.

Layton, my friend Lazarovitch,
no Jew was ever lost
while we two dance joyously
in this French province,
cold and oceans west of the temple,
the snow canyoned on the twigs
like forbidden Sabbath manna;
I say no Jew was ever lost
while we weave and billow the handkerchief
into a burning cloud,
measuring all of heaven
with our stitching thumbs.

Reb Israel Lazarovitch,
you no-good Roumanian, you're right!
Who cares whether or not
the Messiah is a Litvak?
As for the cynical,
such as we were yesterday,
let them step with us or rot
in their logical shrouds.
We've raised a bright white flag,
and here's our battered fathers' cup of wine,
and now is music
until morning and the morning prayers
lay us down again,
we who dance so beautifully
though we know that freilachs end.

Lines from My Grandfather's Journal

I am one of those who could tell every word the pin went through. Page after page I could imagine the scar in a thousand crowned letters. . . .

The dancing floor of the pin is bereft of angels. The Christians no longer want to debate. Jews have forgotten the best arguments. If I spelled out the Principles of Faith I would be barking on the moon.

I will never be free from this old tyranny: "I believe with a perfect faith. . . ."

Why make trouble? It is better to stutter than sing. Become like the early Moses: dreamless of Pharaoh. Become like Abram: dreamless of a longer name. Become like a weak Rachel: be comforted, not comfortless. . .

There was a promise to me from a rainbow, there was a covenant with me after a flood drowned all my friends, inundated every field: the ones we had planted with food and the ones we had left untilled.

Who keeps promises except in business? We were not permitted to own land in Russia. Who wants to own land anywhere? I stare dumbfounded at the trees. Montreal trees, New York trees, Kovno trees. I never wanted to own one. I laugh at the scholars in real estate. . . .

Soldiers in close formation. Paratroops in a white Tel Aviv street. Who dares disdain an answer to the ovens? Any answer.

I did not like to see the young men stunted in the Polish ghetto. Their curved backs were not beautiful. Forgive me, it gives me no pleasure to see them in uniform. I do not thrill to the sight of Jewish battalions.

But there is only one choice between ghettos and battalions, between whips and the weariest patriotic arrogance. . . .

I wanted to keep my body free as when it woke up in Eden.
I kept it strong. There are commandments.

Erase from my flesh the marks of my own whip. Heal the
razor slashes on my arms and throat. Remove the metal
clamps from my fingers. Repair the bones I have crushed in
the door.

Do not let me lie down with spiders. Do not let me en-
courage insects against my eyes. Do not let me make my
living nest with worms or apply to my stomach the comb of
iron or bind my genitals with cord.

It is strange that even now prayer is my natural language. . . .

Night, my old night. The same in every city, beside every
lake. It ambushes a thicket of thrushes. It feeds on the houses
and fields. It consumes my journals of poems.

The black, the loss of sun : it will always frighten me. It
will always lead me to experiment. My journal is filled with
combinations. I adjust prayers like the beads of an abacus. . . .

Thou. Reach into the vineyard of arteries for my heart. Eat
the fruit of ignorance and share with me the mist and
fragrance of dying.

Thou. Your fist in my chest is heavier than any bereave-
ment, heavier than Eden, heavier than the Torah scroll. . . .

The language in which I was trained : spoken in despair of
priestliness.

This is not meant for any pulpit, not for men to chant or
tell their children. Not beautiful enough.

But perhaps this can suggest a passion. Perhaps this passion
could be brought to clarify, make more radiant, the standing
Law.

Let judges secretly despair of justice : their verdicts will be
more acute. Let generals secretly despair of triumph; killing
will be defamed. Let priests secretly despair of faith : their
compassion will be true. It is the tension. . . .

My poems and dictionaries were written at night from my desk or from my bed. Let them cry loudly for life at your hand. Let me be purified by their creation. Challenge me with purity.

O break down these walls with music. Purge from my flesh the need to sleep. Give me eyes for your darkness. Give me legs for your mountains. Let me climb to your face with my argument. If I am unprepared, unclean, lead me first to deserts full of jackals and wolves where I will learn what glory or humility the sand can teach, and from beasts the direction of my evil.

I did not wish to dishonour the scrolls with my logic, or David with my songs. In my work I meant to love you but my voice dissipated somewhere before your infinite regions. And when I gazed toward your eyes all the bristling hills of Judaea intervened.

I played with the idea that I was the Messiah. . . .

> I saw a man gouge out his eye,
> hold it in his fist
> until the nursing sky
> grew round it like a vast and loving face.
> With shafts of light
> I saw him mine his wrist
> until his blood filled out the rest of space
> and settled softly on the world
> like morning mist.

Who could resist such fireworks?

> I wrestled hard in Galilee.
> In the rubbish of pyramids
> and strawless bricks
> I felled my gentle enemy.
> I destroyed his cloak of stars.
> It was an insult to our human flesh,
> worse than scars.

If we could face his work, submit it to annotation. . . .

You raged before them
like the dreams of their old-time God.
You smashed your body
like tablets of the Law.
You drove them from the temple counters.
Your whip on their loins
was a beginning of trouble.
Your thorns in their hearts
was an end to love.

O come back to our books.
Decorate the Law with human commentary.
Do not invoke a spectacular death.
There is so much to explain –
the miracles obscure your beauty. . . .

Doubting everything that I was made to write. My dictionaries groaning with lies. Driven back to Genesis. Doubting where every word began. What saint had shifted a meaning to illustrate a parable. Even beyond Genesis, until I stood outside my community, like the man who took too many steps on Sabbath. Faced a desolation which was unheroic, unbiblical, no dramatic beasts.

The real deserts are outside of tradition. . . .

The chimneys are smoking. The little wooden synagogues are filled with men. Perhaps they will stumble on my books of interpretation, useful to anyone but me.

The white tablecloths – whiter when you spill the wine. . . .

Desolation means no angels to wrestle. I saw my brothers dance in Poland. Before the final fire I heard them sing. I could not put away my scholarship or my experiments with blasphemy.

(In Prague their Golem slept.)

Desolation means no ravens, no black symbols. The carcass of the rotting dog cannot speak for you. The ovens have no tongue. The flames thud against the stone roofs. I cannot claim that sound.

Desolation means no comparisons. . . .

"Our needs are so manifold, we dare not declare them."

It is painful to recall a past intensity, to estimate your distance from the Belsen heap, to make your peace with numbers. Just to get up each morning is to make a kind of peace.

It is something to have fled several cities. I am glad that I could run, that I could learn twelve languages, that I escaped conscription with a trick, that borders were only stones in an empty road, that I kept my journal.

Let me refuse solutions, refuse to be comforted. . . .

Tonight the sky is luminous. Roads of cloud repeat themselves like the ribs of some vast skeleton.

The easy gulls seem to embody a doomed conception of the sublime as they wheel and disappear into the darkness of the mountain. They leave the heart, they abandon the heart to the Milky Way, that drunkard's glittering line to a physical god. . . .

Sometimes, when the sky is this bright, it seems that if I could only force myself to stare hard at the black hills I could recover the gulls. It seems that nothing is lost that is not forsaken: The rich old treasures still glow in the sand under the tumbled battlements; wrapped in a starry flag a master-God floats through the firmament like a childless kite.

I will never be free from this tyranny.

A tradition composed of the exuviae of visions. I must resist it. It is like the garbage river through a city: beautiful by day and beautiful by night, but always unfit for bathing.

There were beautiful rules: a way to hear thunder, praise a wise man, watch a rainbow, learn of tragedy.

All my family were priests, from Aaron to my father. It was my honour to close the eyes of my famous teacher.

Prayer makes speech a ceremony. To observe this ritual in the absence of arks, altars, a listening sky: this is a rich discipline.

I stare dumbfounded at the trees. I imagine the scar in a thousand crowned letters. Let me never speak casually.

Inscription for the family spice-box:

> Make my body
> a pomander for worms
> and my soul
> the fragrance of cloves.
>
> Let the spoiled Sabbath
> leave no scent.
> Keep my mouth
> from foul speech.
>
> Lead your priest
> from grave to vineyard.
> Lay him down
> where air is sweet.

JAY
MACPHERSON

Jay Macpherson was born in England in 1931, but moved
west at an early age, first to Newfoundland, then to Ottawa,
where she attended Carleton University, and to Toronto. For
her MA (1955) at the University of Toronto, she wrote a thesis
on "Milton's Pastoral," a subject congenial to her own poetry.
Her early poems appeared in *Contemporary Verse* at the
end of the forties. After publishing *Nineteen Poems* (1952)
and *O Earth Return* (1954), she joined new and old work into
an organized cycle of lyrics called *The Boatman* (Oxford
University Press, 1957). More recent poems are printed in
Poetry, Chicago (September, 1957), and in the first issue of
James Reaney's magazine *Alphabet* (September, 1960).

Eve in Reflection

Painful and brief the act. Eve on the barren shore
Sees every cherished feature, plumed tree, bright grass.
Fresh spring, the beasts as placid as before
Beneath the inviolable glass.

There the lost girl gone under sea
Tends her undying grove, never raising her eyes
To where on the salt shell beach in reverie
The mother of all living lies.

The beloved face is lost from sight,
Marred in a whelming tide of blood :
And Adam walks in the cold night
Wilderness, waste wood.

❖

The Marriage of Earth and Heaven

Earth draws her breath so gently, heaven bends
On her so bright a look, I could believe
That the renewal of the world was come,
The marriage of kind Earth and splendid Heaven.

"O happy pair" – the blind man lifts his harp
Down from the peg – but wait, but check the song.
The two you praise still matchless lie apart,
Thin air drawn sharp between queen Earth and Heaven.

Though I stand and stretch my hands forever
Till my hair grows down my back and my skirt to my
    ankles,
I shall not hear the triumphs of their trumpets
Calling the hopeful in from all the quarters
To the marriage of kind Earth and splendid Heaven.

Yet out of reason's reach a place is kept
For great occasions, with a fat four-poster bed
And a revelling-ground and a fountain showering beer
And a fiddler fiddling fine for folly's children
To riot rings around at the famous wedding
Of quean Earth and her fancy-fellow Heaven.

❖

The Garden of the Sexes

I have a garden closed away
And shadowed from the light of day
Where Love hangs bound on every tree
And I alone go free.

His sighs, that turn the weathers round,
His tears, that water all the ground,
His blood, that reddens in the vine,
These all are mine.

At night the golden apple-tree
Is my fixed station, whence I see
Terrible, sublime and free,
My loves go wheeling over me.

Aiaia

Now from the sanctified island the light descending
With wailing into the dark
Leaves the live tree, the mothers harsh and bending,
The bridebed closed in bark,

Declines, slips fast through the blackened air
Till the cruel deceiver, gentle at last,
Dawns on extinguished eyes whose stars are past,
Laps the fond innocent head in her cradle of care.

❖

The Old Enchanter

The old enchanter who laid down his head
In woman's mazeful lap was not betrayed
By love or doting, though he gave a maid
His rod and book and lies now like the dead.

The world's old age is on us. Long ago,
Shaken by dragons, swamped with sea-waves, fell
The island fortress, drowned like any shell.
This dreamer hears no tales of overthrow,

In childish sleep brass-walled by his own charms.
In Merlin's bosom Arthur and the rest
Sleep their long night; and Arthur's dragon crest
Seems pacified, though in a witch's arms.

The Natural Mother

All the soft moon bends over,
All circled in her arm,
All that her blue folds cover,
Sleeps shadowed, safe and warm.

Then lullaby King David's town,
The shepherds in the snow,
Rough instruments, uneasy crown,
And cock about to crow,

And lullaby the wakeful bird
That mourns upon the height,
The ancient heads with visions stirred,
The glimmering new light;

Long rest to purple and to pall,
The watchers on the towered wall,
The dreamland tree, the waterfall :
Lullaby my God and all.

✤

The Boatman

You might suppose it easy
For a maker not too lazy
To convert the gentle reader to an Ark :
But it takes a willing pupil
To admit both gnat and camel
– Quite an eyeful, all the crew that must embark.

After me when comes the deluge
And you're looking round for refuge
From God's anger pouring down in gush and spout,
Then you take the tender creature
– You remember, that's the reader –
And you pull him through his navel inside out.

That's to get his beasts outside him,
For they've got to come aboard him,
As the best directions have it, two by two.
When you've taken all their tickets
And you've marched them through his sockets,
Let the tempest bust Creation : heed not you.

For you're riding high and mighty
In a gale that's pushing ninety
With a solid bottom under you – that's his.
Fellow flesh affords a rampart,
And you've got along for comfort
All the world there ever shall be, was, and is.

❖

The Ark

ARK TO NOAH

I wait, with those that rest
In darkness till you come,
Though they are murmuring flesh
And I a block and dumb.

Yet when you come, be pleased
To shine here, be shown
Inward as all the creatures
Drawn through my bone.

ARK ARTICULATE

Shaped new to your measure
From a mourning grove,
I am your sensing creature
And may speak for love.

If you repent again
And turn and unmake me,
How shall I rock my pain
In the arms of a tree?

ARK ANATOMICAL

Set me to sound for you
The world unmade,
As he who rears the head
In light arrayed,

That its vision may quicken
Every wanting part
Hangs deep in the dark body
A divining heart.

ARK ARTEFACT

Between me and the wood
I grew in, you stand
Firm as when first I woke
Alive in your hand.

How could you know your love,
If not defined in me,
From the grief of the always wounded,
Always closing sea?

ARK APPREHENSIVE

I am a sleeping body
Hulling down the night,
And you the dream I ferry
To shores of light.

I sleep that you may wake,
That the black sea
May not gape sheer under you
As he does for me.

ARK ASTONISHED

Why did your spirit
Strive so long with me?
Will you wring love from deserts,
Comfort from the sea?

Your dove and raven speed,
The carrion and the kind.
Man, I know your need,
But not your mind.

ARK OVERWHELMED

When the four quarters shall
Turn in and make one whole,
Then I who wall your body,
Which is to me a soul,

Shall swim circled by you
And cradled on your tide,
Who was not even, not ever,
Taken from your side.

ARK PARTING

You dreamed it. From my ground
You raised that flood, these fears.
The creatures all but drowned
Fled your well of tears.

Outward the fresh shores gleam
Clear in new-washed eyes.
Fare well. From your dream
I only shall not rise.

❖

Leviathan

Now show thy joy, frolic in Angels' sight
Like Adam's elephant in fields of light.
There lamb and lion slumber in the shade,
Splendour and innocence together laid.

The Lord that made Leviathan made thee
Not good, not great, not beautiful, not free,
Not whole in love, not able to forget
The coming war, the battle still unmet.

But look : Creation shines, as that first day
When God's Leviathan went forth to play
Delightful from his hand. The brute flesh sleeps,
And speechless mercy all that sleeping keeps.

❖

Of Creatures the Net

i

Of creatures the net and chain
Stretched like that great membrane
The soft sore ocean
Is by us not broken;

And like an eye or tongue
Is wet and sensing;
And by the ends drawn up
Will strain but not snap.

ii

And in all natures we
The primitive he and she
Carry the child Jesus,
Those suffering senses

That in us see and taste,
With us in absence fast,
For whose scattered and bound
Sake we are joined.

iii

Of the seas the wide cup
Shrinks to a water-drop,
The creatures in its round
As in an eye contained,

And that eye still the globe
Wherein all natures move,
Still tough the skin
That holds their troubles in.

iv

In all the green flood
More closely binds than blood;
Though windowed like a net
Lets none forget

The forsaken brother
And elder other;
Divided is unbroken,
Draws with the chain of ocean.

The Fisherman

The world was first a private park
Until the angel, after dark,
Scattered afar to wests and easts
The lovers and the friendly beasts.

And later still a home-made boat
Contained Creation set afloat,
No rift nor leak that might betray
The creatures to a hostile day.

But now beside the midnight lake
One single fisher sits awake
And casts and fights and hauls to land
A myriad forms upon the sand.

Old Adam on the naming-day
Blessed each and let it slip away :
The fisher of the fallen mind
Sees no occasion to be kind,

But on his catch proceeds to sup;
Then bends, and at one slurp sucks up
The lake and all that therein is
To slake that hungry gut of his,

Then whistling makes for home and bed
As the last morning breaks in red;
But God the Lord with patient grin
Lets down his hook and hoicks him in.

Like Adamant

I thought there was no second Fall,
That I with Eve fell once for all :
But worse succeeds, I no more doubt,
Since heaven-dwellers make me out
First fallen, last obstructive grown,
Like Adamant the wounded stone.

For Adamant with Adam fell
From diamond clear to black as hell,
Though not from heaven dropped so far
As the imperious angels are,
But lies malignant in the sea,
Drawing by its infirmity.

Reader, my sound one, why should you
Hate me, or fear what I might do?
Since Adamant, as is well known,
In whom the wounds of love are shown,
Threatens the man of iron alone,
And not the man of flesh, nor stone.

ALDEN
NOWLAN

Alden Nowlan was born at Windsor, Nova Scotia, in 1933. He left high school early and in 1952 moved to New Brunswick, where he is now News Editor of the Hartland *Observer*. He was awarded a Canada Council Junior Arts Fellowship in 1961. His poems first attracted attention in Canada in the pages of the *Fiddlehead*, which also printed a pamphlet of his work called *The Rose and the Puritan* (1958). A second pamphlet, *A Darkness in the East*, appeared in California the following year. A very prolific writer, Nowlan's poetry has achieved wide circulation in a great variety of North American magazines. More recent books are *Under the Ice* (The Ryerson Press, 1961), *Wind in a Rocky Country* (Emblem Books, 1961) and *The Things Which Are* (Contact Press, 1962). He has also published a number of short stories.

When Like the Tears of Clowns

When like the tears of clowns the rain intrudes
Upon our ordered days and children chant,
Like repetitious birds, their sexless shrill :
My heart crawls lean and lewd, a shrinking thing,
To haylofts where, when I was ten and whipt,
Tall horses swore fidelity and drummed
As wolf-thoughts howled within my punished wrists.

There in the seasoned hay's unsubtle tang
The lash of fleshly pride unleashed my lips

And in a dream I saw the meek bequeathed
Their deep and narrow heritage of earth.

❖

Beginning

From that they found most lovely, most abhorred,
my parents made me : I was born like sound
stroked from the fiddle to become the ward
of tunes played on the bear-trap and the hound.

Not one, but seven entrances they gave
each to the other, and he laid her down
the way the sun comes out. Oh, they were brave,
and then like looters in a burning town

Their mouths left bruises, starting with the kiss
and ending with the proverb, where th^y stayed;
never in making was there brighter bliss,
followed by darker shame. Thus I was made.

Refuge at Eight

Darkness, the smell of earth, the smell of apples,
the cellar swallowed me, I dreamt I died,
saw both blind parents mad with guilt and sorrow,
my ghost sardonic. Finally, I cried.

❖

Aunt Jane

Aunt Jane, of whom I dreamed the nights it thundered,
was dead at ninety, buried at a hundred.
We kept her corpse a decade, hid upstairs,
where it ate porridge, slept and said its prayers.

And every night before I went to bed
they took me in to worship with the dead.
Christ Lord, if I should die before I wake,
I pray thee Lord my body take.

❖

A Poem for Elizabeth Nancy

Emptied from Eden, I look down
into your eyes like caves behind a torrent,
into the blue-green valleys where the cattle
fatten on clover and grow drunk on apples;

into the house asleep and all the curtains
skittish and white as brides (even the wind
meeting their silence, whispers) and I come
into the house with hands that stink from milking,

into this house of candles where my feet
climbing your stairs like laughter leave me standing
before your door, knowing there's no one there,
knowing your room is bare and not much caring.

❖

Two Strangers

Two strangers, one of whom was I,
shook with a rabbit's queasy cry
suppressed by the quick hangman's hood
in the forest of gallows wood.

For one the child-like scream of death
resounded in his tightened breath,
he knew only the air had cried,
the voice itself had died, had died.

For one the ghostly cry brought back
the exultation of the track.
He tasted in his rearing will
the salt of the climactic kill.

For that breath's space there in the trees
they burned with their identities.
Then finding every echo gone,
still saying nothing, they walked on.

Warren Pryor

When every pencil meant a sacrifice
his parents boarded him at school in town,
slaving to free him from the stony fields,
the meagre acreage that bore them down.

They blushed with pride when, at his graduation,
they watched him picking up the slender scroll,
his passport from the years of brutal toil
and lonely patience in a barren hole.

When he went in the Bank their cups ran over.
They marvelled how he wore a milk-white shirt
work days and jeans on Sundays. He was saved
from their thistle-strewn farm and its red dirt.

And he said nothing. Hard and serious
like a young bear inside his teller's cage,
his axe-hewn hands upon the paper bills
aching with empty strength and throttled rage.

Carl

Nobody has ever seen Carl
when he wasn't smiling.

He grins at cats and hydrants
and a huge, wet, collie-like smile
lights up whenever anybody, no matter who,
speaks to him.

When he's hurt
his smile shrinks a little,
pulls its corners in snugly,
but it doesn't go away.

The Anatomy of Angels

Angels inhabit love songs. But they're sprites
not seraphim. The angel that up-ended
Jacob had sturdy calves, moist hairy armpits,
stout loins to serve the god whom she befriended,

and was adept at wrestling. She wore
a cobra like a girdle. Yet his bone
mending he spent some several tedious weeks
marking the bed they'd shared, with a great stone.

❖

Summer

It's summer yet but still the cold
coils through these fields at dusk, the gray Atlantic
haunting the hollows and a black bitch barking
between a rockpile and a broken fence
out on the hill a mile from town where maybe
a she-bear, groggy with blueberries, listens
and the colt, lonesome, runs in crooked circles.

Marian at the Pentecostal Meeting

Marian I cannot begrudge
    the carnival of God,
the cotton candy of her faith
    spun on a silver rod

to lick in bed; a peaked girl,
    neither admired nor clever,
Christ pity her and let her ride
    God's carousel forever.

❖

God Sour the Milk of the Knacking Wench

God sour the milk of the knacking wench
with razor and twine she comes
to stanchion our blond and bucking bull,
pluck out his lovely plumbs.

God shiver the prunes on her bark of chest,
who capons the prancing young.
Let maggots befoul her alive in bed,
and dibble thorns in her tongue.

Fly on the Blue Table

Fly on the blue table
six legs dance
hesitate
like a typist's fingers
quick and purposeful
yet going nowhere.

There on the blue plateau
it is like walking on water
in a movie
the plastic water
under perpetual static lightning
the blind actor
testing the air with outstretched tremulous hands.

And all of this is nonsense
because I cannot describe your world
in which I only exist as a mountain or a rose
exists in my world.
What watcher
except maybe a spider
speculates on your destination,
your striped ripe pimple of belly
jerking over the blue table.

❖

Dancer

The sun is horizontal, so the flesh
of the near-naked girl bouncing a ball
is netted in its light, an orange mesh
weaving between her and the shadowed wall.

Her body glistening and snake-crescendoes
electric in her lighted muscles, she
pauses before each pitch, then rears and throws
the ball against the darkness, venomously.

The interlocking stones cry out and hurl
the black globe back, all human purpose stript
from its wild passage, and the bounding girl
bolts in and out of darkness after it.

Stumbling in the shadows, scalded blind
each time she whirls to face the sunlight, she
at last restores the pattern of her mind.
But every ball's more difficult to see.

❖

The Grove Beyond the Barley

This grove is too secret : one thinks of murder.
Coming upon your white body (for as yet
I do not know you, therefore have no right
to speak of discovering
you, can address myself
to your body only) seeing the disorder
of your naked limbs, the arms outstretched
like one crucified, the legs bent like a runner's,
it took me less than a second to write a novel :
the husband in the black suit
worn at his wedding, the hired man
in his shirt the colour
of a rooster's comb and, in the end, you
thrown here like an axed colt.
Then I saw your breasts : they are not asleep,

move like the shadows of leaves
stirred by the wind. I hope you do not waken,
before I go; one who chooses
so dark a place
to lie naked
might cry out. The shadows quicken,
I wish you a lover,
dreams of sunlit meadows,
imagine myself a gentle satyr.

❖

The Execution

On the night of the execution
a man at the door
mistook me for the coroner.
"Press," I said.

But he didn't understand. He led me
into the wrong room
where the sheriff greeted me :
"You're late, Padre."

"You're wrong," I told him. "I'm Press."
"Yes, of course, Reverend Press."
We went down a stairway.

"Ah, Mr. Ellis," said the Deputy.
"Press!" I shouted. But he shoved me
through a black curtain.
The lights were so bright
I couldn't see the faces
of the men sitting
opposite. But, thank God, I thought
they can see me!

"Look!" I cried. "Look at my face!
Doesn't anybody know me?"

Then a hood covered my head.
"Don't make it harder for us," the hangman whispered.

❖

The Genealogy of Morals

Take any child dreaming of pickled bones
shelved in a coal-dark cellar understairs
(we are all children when we dream) the stones
red-black with blood from severed jugulars.

Child Francis, Child Gilles went down those stairs,
returned sides, hands and ankles dripping blood,
Bluebeard and gentlest saint. The same nightmares
instruct the evil, as inform the good.

KENNETH
McROBBIE

Kenneth McRobbie was born in England in 1929 and attended Liverpool University before emigrating to Canada, where he did graduate work (MA 1956) at the University of Toronto. Although his degree was in history, his thesis was on the fourteenth-century English poem *Piers Plowman*. He spent two years as Reader at the Institute of Historical Research at the University of London, but is now a member of the Department of History at the University of Manitoba. In 1958 he published a broadsheet called *Jupiter C: Four Poems for the Nuclear Age* and in 1960 a substantial book called *Eyes Without a Face* (Gallery Editions). Some recent poems are printed in *Poetry 62* (The Ryerson Press, 1961).

Caryatids in the Park at Night

Water tears across faces
                 on the iron drinking fountains,
barking of dogs fades in the wind
along routes of the park's October men.
Trains shunt far across the grass
                 and the main line smoulders
nearer the mouth's rigor mortis.
They see the thing over there – Time – pass.

The disaster of damp flays the caryatids
                 whose faces peel into the breathing plants.
Lips and brows are crumbling
                 upon those classic simulcra almost
indistinguishable from winter strollers,
                 the skeleton decoratively
suggested at sunset in the hanged gates
                 or a shattered tennis party awaiting
the ball tossed from shadows by a stranger.

And over there, two virtuosos freeze
                 in the arms of a bandstand
marooned on the noisy grass, lips
                 lashed to sudden stone in headlights.
Lost races send the lonely walkers
                 once too often round the Memorial
where wind saturates the spouting faces,
and statues are sweating it out
                 under the trees like men.

Diary of a Nerve

Monday's run on biographies significant.
Caught a librarian crying.
                     It was not
Clear why the old men seized the Reference Room.
Too-long cigarette ends in too-full plates.
Mother acting strange. Mustn't
                 sleep in so late.

Tuesday proves the library is affected.
Breathing from *that* room.
                  So I fled
When operators sang in the mortal exchanges,
And something moved in the catalogue.
Current failing in the suburbs,
                 the wires sob.

Wednesday, Wednesday. I'll always remember
Youths in their crawl stroke surging
                once the girls' wonder
Now drafted into requisitioned rooming houses,
Their wood-green pool forgotten at high tide
As they add and write, the nervous
               sea's skin beside.

Advertisers move out, silencing Thursday.
The smudged news worries
                caretakers by
Stair lights burning in the glass stories.
Paint flakes from all late model cars.
Exhausts obliterate
               sidewalks, stars.

Should have heard of this before Friday
               in order to –

How bones were found gnawed by the campfire,
Weapons within reach.
                        No one can get through now.
The cat has broken all its legs.
I'm alone in a room.
                        Who will read this?

It's today. All cover the beaches with no word.
The freighter from horizon heaving
                        enters the fiord.
The quay falls to a strange cheering.
A bell rings once in the deserted
                        downstairs – and no more,
As I turn at last
                        to look at my stirring door.

❖

The Movement of the Worlds

If I saw only summer's semi-circled
        space mileage in the
                clear half inch of ice
I broke from the black twig
        warm to my touch
                stepping from the cold night
rubber shoed, sweater
        pulled wool over my head
                I felt the first part of me
to touch earth
        my mouth on her's
                release a sharp
flower of electricity
        making us start apart
            – but for a moment
only, for it was winter
        and we knew that we
                must guarantee the sun.

An Insect

An insect
        through the morning
                using his
electric razor
        in the summer-
                shot tree,
shaving
        with a very
                sharp mirror
in which my
        half face calls
                out to him:
How much better
        that you cannot
                cut yourself
on those
        beautiful wings
                you can
never admire!

✤

On Seeing My Name Painted on the Signboard of a Remote Quarry

Out of the driving mirror drives my grave's face
Where my growing hair and nails cover
        In the dark
The eyes' light years.

My limbs meet my name in a limestone quarry
And another's, who made here something but now
    Dries on this
Board by a lake.

As he kicked a seed against the glare of hours
Where he lies, I kick the accelerator away
    Into the life
Laid down by roads.

Out of the past drives the mirror of my name's face
With blood upon it from the grave already, feeding
    The circles
Of his trees.

❖

The World of De Chirico –
after André Breton

We cannot tell the hour, for these
elongated shadows across the square are not those of sundials,
beneath the arches of colonnades they are mystery.
Against the horizon's infinity a train moves
towards Nowhere, releasing phantom plumes of smoke.

Beyond the mobile equestrian statue
which has stood at the edge of the square for so long
that one has forgotten whom it commemorates,
the sea lies waiting for the hour when it shall rise
to overwhelm the dead and empty city.
Roman soldiers wander
and terrific horses gallop over the sands.

We enter the colonnade and find our way into
a white-washed room.
Here there are plaster casts of heads of a type of beauty
now extinct, there are gloves, T-squares, laths
picture-frames, handles of violins
biscuits and strangely marked wands.

Coming towards us from the doorway
with slow, agonising movements
is a menacing and abnormally tall figure, swathed,
its head featureless as an egg, with bricks, scaffoldings
models of buildings and little arches
tumbling from its dreadful breast.
  Its arm creaks as it raises its rubber hand
to point at us, meaninglessly . . .

❖

The White Writing

The women would cover their faces
   with fifteen-year hands, laughing or in grief
   old enough
        (even she for whom since
     all gas rings flame beneath baths of milk,
   Helen's sea passage upon all those brows too
   rising from their hands again through history.

Now the women are abolishing their faces
   as they walk *New World Street*, city of crosses
   cheeks first to vanish in soft lines cloud
      hair thrust high after.
                    A waiter sweeps bare the cold tables
   where one Celine in a cellar bar snatches away
   her hand in dark English, crisp Polish ears
      dissolving, light through her fine gristle of nose.

And for a husband at the crane's controls, coughing
      air white with cement, shall
she not, Krystyna, manipulate the white pencils
    take into her features his world of space
    in the straw choirs kneel among ghosts igniting
    glasses of vodka to the Black Virgin of Czestochowa
At the windows the women hide their faces
    even from old men, revenge they do not understand
      unveiling their bodies
                    to concepts of desire.
The September leathers, water grey wools
are as nothing to bodies freed by technology
    only to suffer intelligently,
    inflating their breasts with paraffin
    who might have smiled on a half-century.
The old men cannot meet the gaze of their country
where death comes as a young woman.

The women disintegrate their faces
    never to rest in hands never at rest
    returning to them each morning marbled with sleep.
      They sit beside the Vistula, white with dawn
    (great cloud shadow leans from the boar forests
    remembering wild strawberries hard as pistol bullets
    turning to wordless smoke in whorls of mouth.

All that remains of the women's faces
    is the rainswept national places, the weight
of sky upon the copper eyeballs of Copernicus
    in the street
               where they make a last stand, in
    eyes, their eyes lined with fierce black
raising that space of which they have made faces
to dark stars known by radiation.
    And when the white writings
quite fill the lines of forgotten smiles
      birds sip the sweetness of their tears
      in the intense dark before daybreak
    going out from their hands after
from souls, how beautiful after snowstorms.

The Decorations of Last Christmas

On a grey pillow
the old lady watches the last holly
                flame, white and
hold shape.

                I bring brandy
to dull her bright eyes
                meat pastes for muscle
in the voice wandering from accidents
                to design, grateful
for the wide hat in the sepia photo
that it survived, clattering
                upon the wall
when direct hit broke out
                the war-time grass, thankful
for the price of cream for pain.

Things go soft, give
                        in her, beneath,
dark aunts pull at her, clothes lack shape,
the fire is too much for her.
                She dreams of emulsions
firm at thirty
                her long ears hard, of cold
fields of still, white, standing sheep.

In her hand, shaping
                        those great shading hats
                one last red berry,
closing on the marks of fruit.
                Ashen decorations
tremble upon the hearth
                        warm, without substance.

This is an anthology of the forties and fifties, and its poets
have been included on the basis of their work during the
period 1940–1960. But no rigid deadline of 1960 was set for
determining the eligibility of the poems themselves. A good
many poems chosen, although written earlier, were first
published since 1960. Others were both written and published
after that date, and a few are taken from the author's
unpublished manuscript.

EARLE BIRNEY. The arrangement of the poems is approximately chronological. The first eight belong to the forties
(except for the earlier "Slug in Woods"), the next three
were collected in 1952 and the next eight in 1962. The last
two are taken from the manuscript of Birney's next
collection. Where "World Winter" (formerly "War
Winter"), "Vancouver Lights," "Anglosaxon Street,"
"David," "Mappemounde," "Ulysses," "Biography," and
"St Valentine Is Passed" differ from previously printed
versions, the changes are in accordance with Birney's most
recent revisions.

IRVING LAYTON. The first three poems were published in the
forties and the last seven since 1960. The arrangement of the
whole is approximately chronological.

MARGARET AVISON. The first three poems were published in
the forties. The last four are more recent than Miss Avison's
only collection (1960), and the last two are previously
unprinted.

RAYMOND SOUSTER. The arrangement of the poems is
approximately in the order of book publication. The first
four appeared in the forties and the last nine (except for
"Invocation to the Muse") in 1962.

JAMES REANEY. The first twelve poems were written within
two or three years (on either side) of Reaney's first book *The*

Red Heart (1949), although only four of them ("The Katzenjammer Kids," "Antichrist as a Child," "Rewards for Ambitious Trees," and "The Royal Visit") are actually to be found in that volume. The first two poems are here printed in the revised and extended versions first published in *Twelve Letters* (1962). The eclogues were written for the set of pastorals published in 1958, and the last three poems have appeared more recently. But Reaney's processes of composition and publication make any chronological arrangement misleading.

P. K. PAGE. The first four poems were published in the poet's 1946 collection and the others in her 1954 one.

LEONARD COHEN. "Story" is an early poem and "On the Sickness of My Love" a recent one; the rest belong to the late fifties and were collected in 1961.

JAY MACPHERSON. All the poems are taken from *The Boatman* (1957), except for the more recent "Of Creatures the Net" and "Like Adamant."

ALDEN NOWLAN. The first poem is from Nowlan's first (1958) collection and the last four from his most recent (1962) one. "Two Strangers," first collected in 1958, is here printed in the revised version of 1961.

KENNETH MCROBBIE. All of these poems were collected in 1960, with the exception of the last two, which are more recent.

Acknowledgements

We wish to thank the following authors, publishers, and copyright holders for their kind permission to reproduce the poems in this book.

MARGARET AVISON: for "Valiant Vacationist," originally published in *Canadian Forum*, and "The Iconoclasts" and "Perspective," originally published in *Poetry*, Chicago; "The Local & the Lakefront" "Waking Up," originally published in *Origin*; and "Holiday Plans for the Whole Family" and "Simon (finis)."

EARLE BIRNEY: for selections from *The Strait of Anian* (The Ryerson Press); and "For George Lamming," and "Plaza del Inquisicion."

LEONARD COHEN: for "Story," originally published in *Let Us Compare Mythologies* (McGill Poetry Series, 1956), and "On the Sickness of My Love," from *Poetry 62* (The Ryerson Press).

MCCLELLAND AND STEWART LIMITED and EARLE BIRNEY: for selections from *Ice Cod Bell or Stone*.

MCCLELLAND AND STEWART LIMITED and LEONARD COHEN: for selections from *The Spice-Box of Earth*.

MCCLELLAND AND STEWART LIMITED and IRVING LAYTON: for selections from *A Red Carpet for the Sun*, *The Swinging Flesh*, and *Balls for a One-Armed Juggler*.

JAY MACPHERSON: for "Of Creatures the Net," originally published in *The Fiddlehead*, and "Like Adamant," originally published in *Poetry*, Chicago.

KENNETH MCROBBIE: for selections from *Eyes Without a Face* (Gallery Editions); and "The White Writing" and "The Decorations of Last Christmas," from *Poetry 62* (The Ryerson Press).

ALDEN NOWLAN: for selections from *Wind in a Rocky Country* (Emblem Books) and *The Things Which Are*; and "Fly on the Blue Table," originally published in *The Fiddlehead*.

THE OXFORD UNIVERSITY PRESS: for "Eve in Reflection," "The Marriage of Earth and Heaven," "The Garden of the Sexes," "Aiaia," "The Old Enchanter," "The Natural Mother," "The Boatman" "The Ark," "Leviathan," and "The Fisherman" from *The Boatman* by Jay Macpherson.

P. K. PAGE: for selections from *As Ten As Twenty* (The Ryerson Press), and *The Metal and the Flower* (McClelland and Stewart Limited).

JAMES REANEY: for selections from *Twelve Letters to a Small Town* (The Ryerson Press), *The Red Heart* (McClelland and Stewart Limited), *A Suit of Nettles*, and *The Killdeer and Other*

Plays (The Macmillan Company of Canada); "The Gramophone," originally published in *Northern Review*, "The Death of the Poet" and "Platonic Love," originally published in *Contemporary Verse*, "The Birth of Venus" and "The Dead Rainbow," originally published in *Here and Now*, "The Horn," originally published in *Queen's Quarterly*, "The Tall Black Hat," originally published in *Canadian Forum*, and "Le Tombeau de Pierre Falcon" from *Poetry 62* (The Ryerson Press).

THE RYERSON PRESS: for "Bushed," "Biography," and "St Valentine Is Past" from *Trial of a City and Other Poems* by Earle Birney; "Search" from *Unit of Five*, and "Night Watch" and "Poem for Her Picture" from *Go To Sleep World* by Raymond Souster; "When Like the Tears of Clowns," "Beginning," "Refuge at Eight," "Aunt Jane," "A Poem for Elizabeth Nancy," "Two Strangers," "Warren Pryor," "Carl," and "The Anatomy of Angels" from *Under the Ice* by Alden Nowlan.

RAYMOND SOUSTER: for selections from *Selected Poems* (Contact Press), *Place of Meeting* (Gallery Editions), *A Local Pride* (Contact Press), and *Crepe-Hanger's Carnival*.

THE UNIVERSITY OF TORONTO PRESS: for "From a Provincial," "New Year's Poem," "Voluptuaries and Others," "All Fools' Eve," "Snow," "Butterfly Bones; or Sonnet Against Sonnets," "Meeting Together of Poles and Latitudes (in-Prospect)," "Mordent for a Melody," "On the Death of France Darte Scott," "Birth Day," "Dispersed Titles," "To Professor X, Year Y," "Intra-Political," and "Thaw" from *Winter Sun* by Margaret Avison.

SELECTED NEW CANADIAN LIBRARY TITLES

Asterisks (*) denote titles of New Canadian Library Classics